Gage reached for her hand.

"Kate, I saw your face when you were looking at those baby pictures. That's what you want for yourself, isn't it? A husband, babies, a family?"

She didn't answer right away. Instead, she held his gaze, tears slipping free from her eyelashes and trickling down her cheek. Each tear was a sucker punch to his gut, because they confirmed what he'd known all along. Kate wanted things he couldn't give her. How could a tormented ex-soldier, who'd seen and done things that still gave him nightmares, ever give a woman with a pure heart like Kate's any kind of stability or happiness?

D0824212

Dear Reader,

In March of last year, I had the pleasure of having dinner with Harlequin Romantic Suspense Senior Editor Patience Smith (now Bloom) at a writers' conference in Florida. One of the things we talked about was how much fun Patience had had creating Donald and Bonnie Gene Kelley, based on her own parents, for The Coltons of Montana continuity. Later in the dinner, the conversation turned to what might be done with a new continuity. Patience was ready to move away from the Coltons for a while and was thinking of creating a new family dynasty.

"Why not use the Kelleys?" I asked, and Patience's face brightened. Voilà! The Kelleys continuity was born.

I've had a terrific time working on this latest miniseries and hope you'll enjoy Gage and Kate's story as much as I did. Thank you to Laurie Emerson for lending her name to my story and to Lauren Murray for sharing her cat, Sinatra. Each of these ladies won the opportunity by having the high bid in the Brenda Novak Auction for Diabetes last May for their respective auction item.

Watch for more chances to share your name with a character or have your cat featured in one of my upcoming books!

Best wishes and happy reading,

Beth Cornelison

Watch out for these other books in the riveting new Kelley Legacy miniseries:

Private Justice by Marie Ferrarella—July 2011
Cowboy Under Siege by Gail Barrett—September 2011
Rancher Under Cover by Carla Cassidy—October 2011
Missing Mother-to-Be by Elle Kennedy—November 2011
Captain's Call of Duty by Cindy Dees—December 2011

BETH
CORNELISON

Special Ops Bodyguard

ROMANTIC
SUSPENSE

Special thanks and acknowledgment to Beth Cornelison for
her contribution to The Kelley Legacy miniseries.

Recycling programs
for this product may
not exist in your area.

ISBN-13: 978-0-373-27738-4

SPECIAL OPS BODYGUARD

Books by Beth Cornelison

BETH CORNELISON

started writing stories as a child when she penned a tale about the adventures of her cat, Ajax. A Georgia native, she received her bachelor's degree in public relations from the University of Georgia. After working in public relations for a little more than a year, she moved with her husband to Louisiana, where she decided to pursue her love of writing fiction.

Since that first time, Beth has written many more stories of adventure and romance suspense and has won numerous honors for her work, including a coveted Golden Heart award in romantic suspense from Romance Writers of America. She is active on the board of directors for the North Louisiana Storytellers and Authors of Romance (NOLA STARS) and loves reading, traveling, *Peanuts'* Snoopy and spending downtime with her family.

She writes from her home in Louisiana, where she lives with her husband, one son and two cats who think they are people. Beth loves to hear from her readers. You can write to her at P.O. Box 5418, Bossier City, LA 71171 or visit her website at www.bethcornelison.com.

Thanks to Patience Bloom for the opportunity
to contribute to the Kelleys!

To my son, Jeffery—you make me so proud!

Chapter 1

If experience had taught Gage Prescott anything, it was that looks could be deceiving. An isolated and empty road in Afghanistan could be hiding IEDs and well-camouflaged Taliban fighters. Even on a quiet evening, an ambush and the slaughter of your team could happen in blinding seconds.

Likewise, Maple Cove, a sleepy Montana town nestled at the foot of the Absaroka Mountains in the shadow of Mount Cowen, might not be the safe escape his client was looking for. The U.S. Senator from California, Henry "Hank" Kelley, had retreated to his son Cole's ranch just outside the idyllic-looking small town after riling his enemies and having numerous mistresses come forward alleging affairs. Hank Kelley's life was in shambles, and the senator feared for it— which was why his son Dylan had hired Gage and another bodyguard to protect his father.

While Bart Holden, Hank's other bodyguard, had the night

shift guarding the senator, Gage had taken the opportunity to do a little reconnaissance.

He parked the ancient pickup truck he'd borrowed from the ranch hands and sent an all encompassing glance around the main street of Maple Cove. He half expected to see a whistling man and his son strolling down the street with fishing poles, à la Mayberry.

A yellow moon rose above the jagged mountains and cast an eerie glow over the red maple trees lining the main street. In the dim evening light, the fall foliage took on a blood-red cast, and images of gore and the cacophony of gunfire and agonized screams prodded his memory. His heart thundering and a fine sheen of sweat rising above his lip, Gage squeezed the steering wheel and shook off the haunting sights and sounds.

This quiet hamlet was a far cry from the barren and dangerous landscape where he'd last worked, but the chill in the October evening air burrowed into Gage's bones and warned him all might not be as calm and safe as it seemed.

Slamming the truck door behind him, Gage headed down the sidewalk, getting a feel for the town. As he passed a small diner, the aroma of fresh baked bread and savory beef wafted out to the street, and his stomach rumbled. Deciding Ira's Diner was a good place to start meeting the town's citizens and scoping out potential hazards for the senator, Gage stepped inside. When the bell over the door announced his arrival, a blond waitress behind the counter looked up from the register's cash drawer and shot him a smile filled with sunshine.

"Hello there," the honey haired vision said, her lilting voice as bright as her smile. "Make yourself at home. I'll be right over to get your order."

Gage arched an eyebrow, intrigued by the beautiful waitress. He wasn't sure what sort of women he'd expected to find in the small town, but this perky blonde certainly hadn't been on his radar. He chose a stool at the lunch counter and picked up the sticky menu to peruse the diner's offerings.

"Howdy, stranger. What brings you to our humble town?" The blonde slid a glass of ice water in front of him and used a rag to wipe the counter.

Gage glanced up from the menu, and his breath caught in his lungs. The waitress's wheat colored hair was streaked with gold and framed eyes as clear and blue as the Montana sky. For a moment, he could only stare, his body humming with a purely male interest he hadn't experienced in more months than he could count.

"Sir? Everything all right?"

Her question nudged him from his daze, and he frowned, embarrassed to have been caught gawking. "Yeah, fine. I'll, uh…have the roast beef and potatoes. Coffee. Black."

He handed the menu back to her, and she grinned. "Good choice. The beef around here is the best you've ever had. Guaranteed." She scribbled his order on a pad, then hung the sheet on the order wheel for the kitchen. "One of the advantages of living in ranching country. Prime beef."

He tipped his head in acknowledgment but kept his expression neutral. "What are the advantages if you're a vegetarian?"

She sputtered a laugh, and the twinkle of amusement in her gaze made his pulse dance a little two-step. "Then I guess you'd have to find your pleasure in the scenic beauty and the friendly people of our fine state."

"I agree the *scenery*—" he paused meaningfully and lifted one eyebrow "—here is more beautiful than I'd expected."

Her eyes narrowed, but her lopsided grin kept her expression light. "Why, sir, are you flirting with me?"

Gage pressed his lips in a hard line just short of a scowl.

"I don't flirt, ma'am. If I were interested in you, I'd let you know. No games."

She rocked back on her heels, and her smile faded. "Oh, I— Sorry." She seemed inordinately rattled by his gruff response. An endearing pink tint filled her ivory cheeks, and she caught her plump bottom lip with her teeth. She was sexy innocence personified, and he felt like a first-class heel for his curt reply.

Flapping a hand toward the other end of the counter, she took a step back. "I'll just…get your coffee."

Gage gritted his teeth as she hurried away, leaving the scent of vanilla and cinnamon in her wake. He savored the sweet aroma and kicked himself for driving her away. What was wrong with him? Just because he was on assignment and had no business entertaining any ideas of female company didn't mean he couldn't be friendly. Or at least civil. People didn't generally use the term *friendly* in regards to him. He didn't do warm and fuzzy. Two tours in Afghanistan with the U.S. Army Rangers had hardened him, jaded him. His last mission had scarred him. Both physically and mentally. He found it hard to be hearts and flowers when his best friends' blood was on his hands, and the dying moans of his Rangers team echoed in his nightmares.

Still, his lousy past wasn't her fault, and he might need an ally in town, a resource for information about the people and politics in Maple Cove. Perhaps a better tactical move would be to enlist her help rather than keep the tempting treat at arms' length.

She set a steaming mug in front of him but offered no smile this time. "Coffee. Black."

"Thanks," he grunted, and before he could form a question about the residents of the town, she'd spun away and returned to the far end of the counter.

Sighing, Gage turned his stool so he could lean back

against the counter on his elbows and take in the rest of the diner. The buttery-yellow walls and high ceiling lent the otherwise dark decor a feminine touch, much the way his perky waitress had shone her light on his grim mood tonight. He angled a side glance toward her and caught her furtive glance in his direction. Jerking her gaze away, she ducked her head, blushing to her roots, and gave the counter a harder wipe.

Gage's cheek twitched in an almost grin. She so blatantly wore her heart on her sleeve, he wanted to laugh. Her openness and lack of pretense was refreshing.

Looks could be deceiving.

He groaned internally. Always staying guarded, wary and suspicious grew tiresome, but in Gage's world, relaxing your defenses or showing your deeper self meant leaving yourself open to attack. Weak. *Vulnerable.*

Near the diner's door, an elderly gentleman scraped the last bite of pie from his plate while reading a Bozeman newspaper. "Delicious as always, Kate!" he called to the blonde, who responded with a wide grin.

A few tables away, a young couple with a whiny baby packed up their belongings and called a good night to the cook through the open kitchen door. Across the room, another waitress, also an attractive blonde, though not in the same league as Miss Sunshine, wiped tables, then sent him a curious look as she carried a tray of dirty dishes from the dining room.

"Order up, Kate," the cook called as he slapped a plate up on the shelf under the order wheel.

Miss Sunshine scurried over, flashed the cook a bright smile, and called, "Thanks, Pete."

She gathered a set of silverware and a napkin before she carried Gage's dinner to him.

"Can I get you anything else?" She added a quick smile, though the light didn't reach her eyes.

You hurt her.

He shook his head, and as she turned to leave, he said, "Business."

She faced him, a curious crease in her brow. "Pardon?"

"You asked me earlier what brought me to town. I'm here on business. On assignment."

Her expression warmed, clearly taking his answer as the apology he intended. Following his cue, she leaned her hip against the counter, and her smile lit with the sunshine with which she'd first greeted him. "What kind of assignment? Are you a reporter?"

He cut himself a bite of the beef and shook his head. "Security specialist."

She blinked at him. "Which means…what?"

"I'm protecting a client."

Her eyebrows shot up, and her cornflower eyes widened. "As in a bodyguard? Who for?" She leaned closer, lowering her voice to a titillated hush. "Is there a movie star in town?"

He shoved the meat in his mouth. "No. Not a movie star." The tender beef and perfect seasoning of his dinner registered as he chewed, and he couldn't suppress the groan of pure satisfaction.

His waitress's grin turned smug. "Told you it was the best you'd ever have. And wait until you try my apple pie. I just took it out of the oven before you walked in here. I'll cut you a fat slice if you'd like."

Gage stabbed another bite. "Maybe."

"Wait a minute." She sent him a speculative look. "Cole Kelley's dad is a U.S. Senator." She tucked a handful of silky, honey blond hair behind her ear and canted toward him. "So… is it Senator Kelley? Is that who you're protecting?"

Gage cut a glance toward her as he launched into the creamiest mashed potatoes he'd ever eaten. "You know Cole?"

Even though he avoided answering her question directly,

he knew by the lift in her blond eyebrow that she'd deduced she was correct.

"Everyone in Maple Cove knows Cole. He runs the Bar Lazy K ranch. He comes in here to eat pretty regularly— especially on Thursdays when I make chocolate layer cake. Great guy. Handsome, too."

A pinprick of jealousy jabbed Gage, though why he cared about her opinion of Cole Kelley's looks, he couldn't say. He wasn't in town to get involved with any of the locals. He had a job to do, and when he finished that job, he'd leave Maple Cove. No attachments, no entanglements.

"And I understand he has a twin brother in California who's a silent partner in the Bar Lazy K," she added.

Gage nodded. "Dylan."

He'd been fully briefed on the whole extended Kelley clan and their roots here in Montana. Henry's brother Donald had started Kelley's Cookhouse, a barbecue restaurant that had flourished and become a nationwide chain.

The other waitress bustled through the kitchen door and headed their way. "Kate, if we're going to get out of here any time soon, you need to stop pestering the customers and get this counter in order."

Kate. Gage made a mental note of the name the other waitress had called Miss Sunshine. He hitched his head toward the other end of the counter. "You go on. I don't want to get you in trouble with your boss."

Kate snorted. "She's not my boss. She's just bossy," she said, loudly enough for the other woman to hear. "That's my older sister, Janet, and I'm Kate Rogers."

Janet sauntered over and snapped a damp dish towel at Kate's bottom. "Who are you calling bossy, brat?"

Kate laughed, the sound as musical as wind chimes. A sweet thrill raced through Gage's veins, and he gritted his teeth, suppressing his reaction to Kate.

Get a grip, soldier. What was it about this woman that made him wax poetical like some lame…well, poet? Sure, she was pretty and friendly and a refreshing change from the ball buster sort of women he usually met, but he had no excuse for losing his head around her.

"Janet, this is…uh, I'm sorry. I never got your name."

"Gage Prescott." He offered his hand to Janet, and they shook. When he would have withdrawn his hand, Janet clung to his fingers, meeting his eyes with a come-hither look that startled him. Her lack of subtlety was bad enough, but when he spotted the wedding ring on her left hand, he became distinctly uncomfortable.

"So, where are you from, handsome?" Janet asked.

"Bozeman, most recently." Giving her a quelling look, Gage extricated his hand, but not before she had let her fingers stroke his palm as she slid her hand from his. He cut a glance to Kate, who either hadn't noticed her sister's behavior or chose to ignore it. "I lived all over the world while I was in the army."

Janet's eyes widened. "Really? Like where? Paris? Rome?"

"Uh, no. More like Baghdad, Manila, Guam."

Janet's expression deflated, then she shot him a horrified look. "Have you ever killed anyone?"

More than I want to think about.

Kate flushed and swatted at her sister. "That's a terrible thing to ask!"

Janet's reply faded to background noise as Gage flashed on the bloody Afghan road where his recon had failed to protect his team from ambush. The deaths of more than a dozen good soldiers, men he called friends, were on his head. Nausea swamped him, and a fine sheen of sweat gathered on his brow.

"So why does Senator Kelley need a bodyguard?" Kate asked, pulling him out of his haunting memory. "And what's he doing in Maple Cove? Last I heard, there was no love lost between him and Cole."

"I'm not at liberty to say. The senator's relationship with his son is only my business as it relates to keeping the senior Kelley safe."

"I saw on the news where all those women came forward claiming he'd had affairs with them." Janet leaned forward, a conspiratorial gleam in her eye. "So is it true? Did he sleep with all those women? What did his wife say?"

Gage scowled. "That's not for me to say."

Kate scooted closer, partially wedging herself between Janet and Gage. "Please excuse my sister, Gage. She failed Tact and Manners 101 in school." She gave her sister a meaningful look. "Don't you have some tables to wipe or something?"

Janet's mouth puckered as if she'd tasted something sour. "No. I've finished my work. Have you?"

Kate sighed her exasperation but plastered on a patient smile. "Almost."

Straightening her shoulders, Kate offered Gage a rueful grin as she turned to gather the sugar dispensers behind the counter.

Studying the two sisters, Gage couldn't help but notice the differences. Both were physically beautiful, yet Janet's attitude toward her sister, her graceless flirting and untoward questions made her unattractive. Kate, on the other hand, had a glow and magnetism that shone from inside, raising her outward appearance to pure radiance. Gage found himself drawn as much to that inner warmth as to her bright blue eyes and feminine curves.

Snatching him from thoughts of her sister, Janet covered Gage's hand with hers and leaned so far toward him, he had a clear view down her shirt. Which, he had no doubt, was her intention. "So, tell me about being a bodyguard."

"I'd rather you ladies tell me about Maple Cove. Working here in the diner, I imagine you know most everyone."

"True enough. What do you want to know?" Janet propped her chin on her hand and braced her elbows on the counter, as if settling in for a juicy round of gossip.

Gage sat back, crossing his arms over his chest and directing his comments as much to Kate as to her sister. "Personalities. Conflicts. Anyone in town have hard feelings toward the Kelleys?"

Janet scrunched her nose as if searching her memory for the best dirt she had on the Kelley family.

"I don't think anyone has a beef against Cole, if that's what you mean. He's well-respected by the other ranchers," Kate said. "I *have* heard some locals disagree with the senator's politics, but nothing extreme. What kind of conflicts do you mean?"

"Just getting a feel for the town. Is there anyone I should be forewarned about, anyone who could be trouble?"

Janet smirked and dragged a fingernail down his chest. "Depends. What kind of trouble you looking to get in?"

The bell over the door jingled, and both Janet's and Kate's eyes darted toward the newcomer. Janet paled, jerking upright and stepping back from Gage, a guilty look on her face. Kate's expression clouded and she visibly tensed.

Alerted to trouble by their reactions to the new arrival, Gage turned on the stool and spotted a wiry man in jeans, boots and a Western shirt—typical ranch-hand garb—stride into the diner with a hard glare pinned on the women. "What the hell's going on in here?"

"Larry," Janet gasped, flicking a nervous glance at the clock. "You're early."

The man glowered at Gage, then at Janet. "Seems to me I'm just in the nick of time. What were you and this clown doing, pawing each other like that?"

"I—I—"

"Nobody was pawing anyone, Larry," Kate said.

He snapped a churlish look toward Kate. "Stay out of this! This is between me and my wife!"

Gage groaned internally. Great. A jealous husband.

Larry stalked behind the counter and grabbed Janet by the arm. "I know what I saw when I came in. Don't lie to me!"

His muscles tensing, Gage lifted a hand, palm out. "Take it easy, pal."

"Honest, honey. Nothing happened. I—" Janet whimpered in pain as her husband squeezed harder on her upper arm and jerked her toward the door.

"I knew I couldn't trust you." He started for the door, dragging Janet, who stumbled along behind him.

Gage bristled and felt a rush of heat flood his face and neck, his jaw tightening.

Kate flew around the counter after her sister. "Wait, Larry. Maybe Janet should stay here for a while." She stepped in Larry's path and placed a gentle hand on his shoulder. "Just until you've had a chance to calm d—"

Larry planted a hand in the middle of Kate's chest and shoved her so hard she fell backward, knocking over several chairs as she tumbled to the floor.

Gage launched off his stool and intercepted Larry at the door, blocking the irate husband's exit. The last thing he wanted was to be distracted from his security job by domestic problems of the local residents, but he couldn't let the jerk's abhorrent treatment of his wife and Kate go unchallenged, either. Abusive husbands ranked somewhere just below sewage scum in his esteem.

"Outta my way, creep," Larry growled.

"I don't think so." Gage crossed his arms over his chest, ready to do battle with the cretin if needed. "Not until you apologize to Kate and let go of your wife's arm."

Larry puffed out his chest and got in Gage's face. "Who the hell do you think you are telling me my business with my wife?"

"Looks like I'm the guy who's going to teach you the right way to treat women."

Hank Kelley stared at the woman on the television screen and ground his back teeth together. Even here in Montana at his son Cole's ranch, he couldn't escape the endless parade of reports blasting his private life to the world. The beautiful blonde now simpering for the cameras and staring back at him from the screen had been a temptation too great to resist while he'd been vacationing in Aspen two years ago. Apparently the Colorado ski resort didn't have the same motto of discretion that Vegas did. Not that his Vegas tryst had "stayed in Vegas" either. So far, six of his affairs had been aired for the media as one willowy blonde after another had come forward, maligning his name and driving another nail into the coffin of his marriage.

Hank rattled the ice in the highball glass he clutched, then tossed back the last gulp of Maker's Mark. If only the women coming out of the woodwork were the worst of his problems. Wiping his mouth with the back of his hand, Hank set the glass aside and used the remote to turn off the TV. Acid swirled in his gut as he considered the dangers that had driven him into hiding. While his mistresses took aim at his reputation, other enemies had threatened his life. Had put his family in the crosshairs.

Just days ago, someone had taken his only daughter, Lana, hostage in an attempt to win his cooperation with a nefarious plot, and his son Dylan had hired two bodyguards to babysit him around the clock. Arrangements had been made for him to come here, to the Bar Lazy K, to hide.

Hide! Like some pathetic rabbit scurrying down a hole

away from a fox. He was a *senator,* damn it! A leader! He hated the idea of holing up in his son's ranch like some cowering wimp. He needed to be doing something to find Lana. To get the wolves off his back. Not hiding at his son's house, no matter how well-protected and secure the ranch was.

Hank gritted his teeth and drummed his fingers on the bedside table.

If only he'd never gone to that meeting of the Raven's Head Society, the highly secretive assembly of powerful men who now had him by the balls, he wouldn't be in this mess. Lana would still be safe in Europe. His career wouldn't be on the line. He wouldn't be constantly looking over his shoulder wondering who he could trust.

Or waiting for the media to flash breaking news that President Joe Colton had been killed and he'd been framed as the chief suspect in the murder conspiracy.

Hindsight might be twenty-twenty, but it provided no solutions—only deep regret. He gritted his teeth and slammed his fist on the bedside table. Dammit, there has to be a way to stop this juggernaut before anyone gets hurt!

Across the room, Bart Holden, his night-duty bodyguard, folded his arms over his barrel chest. "If you're ready to call it a night, I'll give you some privacy. If you need me, I'll be right outside the door. Or you can use the intercom."

Hank cast a side glance to the call button by his bed and jerked a nod. "Good night."

One reason for coming to Cole's ranch rather than lying low somewhere else was Cole's elaborate security system, which Hank's somewhat paranoid mother had installed to protect her vast wealth before selling the property to her grandsons. The entire main house had been wired with an intercom system, the wine cellar had been modified to be a panic room in case of trouble, and security cameras and an alarm system protected each outbuilding and the main house.

But being locked down in a house as secure as Fort Knox didn't ease Hank's mind. Lana was being held hostage. The president was in danger. And past mistakes of every sort had crept out of the shadows to ruin Hank's career and threaten his life.

He had to find a way to stop the Raven's Head Society. And soon.

Kate rubbed her throbbing elbow, which had taken the brunt of her fall, and held her breath as Gage squared off with Larry. This could get ugly.

She glanced toward the kitchen where Pete Greenburg, the cook, would be cleaning pots and pans in preparation for closing. Pete, who had recently celebrated his sixtieth birthday, had expressed his concern for Janet's situation before, but also made it clear he chose to stay out of other people's business. The cook would be of little help if a brawl erupted.

Maybe she should call the local police. Or better yet, since Larry had too many friends in the Maple Cove Police Department, she should call Wes Colton, the county sheriff. Wes had a reputation with the ranchers for being a fair and reliable lawman.

"Let. Go. Of. Her. Arm." Gage grated through clenched teeth. His icy blue eyes lasered into Larry, and veins stood out on his linebacker neck.

Rising slowly from the floor and dusting her hands, Kate studied Gage's glowering countenance and chiseled features. His granite expression brooked no resistance, nor did his unflinching position blocking Larry's escape. Muscled arms, one with a barbed wire tattoo around his bicep, folded across a chest wide enough to more than fill the door.

Kate shivered. If she hadn't seen flashes of good humor from Gage earlier, she'd swear the man was made of rock or steel. Hard. Cold. Surly.

Yet he was defending her and Janet from Larry's rough treatment. Something no other man in Maple Cove had ever done. Larry's buddies on the police force looked the other way every time Kate called them to help Janet. Of course, it didn't help that Janet never pressed charges.

He didn't mean it, Katie. I'm fine. I provoked him. He's sorry, and he promised never to do it again.

Kate was thoroughly sick of Janet's excuses, but what could she do if her sister refused to leave the abusive marriage? Kate would stick by Janet, her only blood relative, as long as it took.

Knowing that this rough-hewn man, this stranger who had found his way to their small town, was taking her side, seeing the situation for what it was and doing something about it, made Kate feel a certain bond with him. As though they were allies in a war.

Even if her ally was rather…brutish and gruff.

He was here, after all, to protect Hank Kelley. That meant he had to be tough. Right? But he was still a good guy. Wasn't he?

"Move your ass," Larry snarled, releasing Janet but not backing down from his opponent.

Gage held firm. "Apologize to Kate for shoving her and to Janet for hurting her arm."

"Bite me." Larry balled his fists.

The dark glare Gage nailed on Larry left a cold dread curling in Kate's stomach. Ally or not, she decided the smart move on her part would be to avoid Gage Prescott while he was in town. She had no room in her life for brutish, grouchy men, even if she had felt a spark of attraction earlier, when he'd cracked his granite facade for an instant. She'd have sworn he was flirting with her, that he'd felt the same crackle of electricity when their eyes had met.

But what did she know about men? She'd never had more

than a few dates before she'd moved to Maple Cove, and the list of available, desirable men in her new home was frighteningly short. Kate had resigned herself to being alone and celibate for the foreseeable future, because she refused to abandon her sister. Somehow she had to save Janet from her bad marriage and poor choices.

A muscle in Gage's square jaw flexed as he gritted his teeth. "Apologize to the ladies. Or we'll still be standing here at breakfast tomorrow morning."

Kate had no doubt Gage had the stamina to outlast Larry in a battle of wills. She stooped to right the chairs she'd knocked over as she fell, but she kept a wary eye on the standoff.

Larry finally huffed a disgusted sigh and turned an angry gaze aside. "Sorry, Kate. Janet."

He cut a sharp look to Gage and cocked his head as if to say, "Well?"

Gage grunted and stepped aside.

Kate hurried over to her sister and stopped her from following Larry out the door. "Don't go yet, Janet. Give him time to cool off."

Janet shook her head. "He won't cool down. He'll just get madder. It's better if I go now."

"Janet!" Larry barked from the sidewalk, "Come on—now, or you're walking home!"

She shrugged and forced a grin for Kate as she headed out. "Don't forget to scrub out the tea urn, Kate. See you in the morning."

Kate's gut knotted, and tears clogged her throat. "Be careful, Janet! I love you!"

The diner door closed with a jangle of bells that seemed mockingly cheerful in light of the tension still vibrating in the air.

Kate stared out the plate glass window long after Janet and Larry had disappeared from view. How was she supposed to convince her sister that Larry wouldn't change? Real love didn't hurt. The promises Larry made and the apologies he piled on his abuse didn't make up for his rough and demeaning treatment when he lost his temper.

"Are you hurt?"

The deep male voice shook her from her troubled thoughts. She spun around to find Gage watching her with those glacier-pale eyes. Wiping her hands on her apron, she managed a grateful smile as she shook her head.

"I'll be fine. Just bumped my elbow."

He stepped toward her as she hurried to the counter to finish cleaning up for closing. When he wrapped his large hand around her wrist, she gasped, as much startled by the electric tingle that raced through her from his touch as by his unexpected approach. "Let me have a look. I'm familiar with first aid."

Kate felt the heat rush to her cheeks, and she silently cursed her Nordic genes that made her flush at the slightest provocation. Having Gage's wall of testosterone towering over her as he gently probed her elbow was more than enough to start butterflies swirling inside her.

"I don't think anything's broken," he murmured as he examined her arm.

"Told you."

When he angled his gaze to meet hers, Kate flashed a teasing grin. He arched one dark eyebrow, and a dizzying combination of attraction and intimidation buffeted her. With his thick, wavy brown hair, broad shoulders and square jaw, Gage definitely had masculine appeal. But his piercing blue eyes and unsmiling mouth rattled her, especially since she didn't have a lot of experience with men to begin with. She didn't fear him, per se. After all, he'd come to Janet's rescue, stood up for them against Larry. His chivalry went a long way, in her book, toward excusing a stern persona.

As if she were looking for a man... Kate gave her head a quick shake. She had no business sizing Gage up. He was only a visitor in town, and until she convinced Janet to leave Maple Cove, perhaps go back to Ohio where they had grown up, she had to make her sister her priority.

Besides, when she chose a man, she'd be looking for someone sweet and warm and kind. Someone safe. No temper-prone Larrys or gruff Gages for her. No thank you!

Gage released her arm and narrowed his eyes. "Tell me about him."

Chapter 2

Kate blinked. She'd been lost in her own thoughts, and Gage's request felt like a non sequitur. "I'm sorry?"

"Your sister's husband. What's his story?"

Kate's shoulders sagged. "Oh. Larry." She puffed her bangs off her forehead as she circled the end of the counter and started putting away silverware. "Well, clearly the guy acts like a jerk sometimes."

His steady gaze held hers, showing no reaction to her comment. He showed little if any emotion at all, in fact. For not the first time, meeting his stoic expression brought to mind the craggy rock cliffs of the surrounding mountains. Hard. Cold. Unmoving.

"Go on," he prodded.

Kate twitched a nervous grin, embarrassed to have been caught staring. *And what about him staring at you?*

"He's not always like that, mind you." Kate sighed and jammed a handful of drinking straws in the dispenser. "By tomorrow he'll be apologizing all over the place and making her promises…" She let her voice trail off, wondering why she was telling this stranger her sister's private business. With a quick, embarrassed grin, she shrugged the topic away.

"And he convinces her to stay."

She cut a startled glance to his and nodded.

"Sounds like typical battered wife syndrome to me."

Battered wife syndrome. A chill raced down Kate's spine. Though she knew the truth about Janet's marriage, hearing the harsh but honest term applied to her sister was unsettling.

"Has she called the police on him?" Gage asked.

Kate hesitated. Did she want to get into this with a man she just met? "Uh, yeah. She has. So have I. For all the good it does." She gnawed her bottom lip and sighed. "Larry went to school with the guys on the force. They're his buddies. They don't do anything about him."

Gage's dark eyebrows drew together, and his light blue eyes turned stormy. His muttered curse rumbled like approaching thunder. Kate's hands stilled on the countertop, and she tipped her head, studying him. "Why do you ask?"

His chin jerked up a notch. "Someone should do something about him. He can't be allowed to hurt her, or you, and get away with it."

"I'm trying to help her. I moved out here from Ohio about a year ago to be with her. She's the only family I have, and I can't let her—" She dropped her gaze to her hands when her voice cracked.

An awkward silence passed, filled only by the clatter of dishes from the kitchen where Pete was preparing for the next morning's breakfast.

"Janet is lucky to have you." The words were spoken so softly, she could almost believe she'd imagined them.

Lifting her head, she met a penetrating stare that seemed more caring now than icy. His pale blue irises were flecked with navy, which warmed his eyes and softened the hard edge he projected.

Or maybe she was just seeing what she wanted to see. Was she so desperate for a man that she'd conjured tenderness and warmth in a stranger who'd yet to crack a smile for her?

Sucking in a deep breath, she rallied herself. "I believe I promised you a piece of my apple pie."

Glad for the distraction, Kate took the pie down from the pastry stand and cut Gage a thick slice. "My best friend in Ohio was the Amish girl who lived next door to us. I learned to bake from her mother. I spent hours with them every day. Spent more time at their farm than at my own house, in fact. Anyway, Emma's mother taught me to cook and people around here seem to think my desserts are pretty good. But judge for yourself."

She slid the pie in front of him and handed him a clean fork.

Gage cut a bite, shoveled it into his mouth and chewed slowly. Kate held her breath, as if his verdict had the power to end or salvage her baking career.

His eyebrows lifted, and he nodded, licking flakes of crust from his lips.

Kate's gaze zeroed in on the quick sweep of his tongue, and a fuzzy warmth swam through her, settling low in her womb. Dear heavens, why did such a simple thing seem... *erotic* to her?

Another flood of heat stung her cheeks. She wasn't used to a man having this sort of effect on her.

After he swallowed, Gage turned the fork in his fingers idly.

"Well?" She canted toward him, all too eager for his assessment.

His stony expression shifted, his lips twisting wryly, and

a sultry heat lighting his eyes. "Only thing I've ever had any better was sex."

"Oh. I—" The heat in her cheeks shot straight to the roots of her hair. Her hand fluttered to her mouth, and she covered a stunned laugh. "I, uh…thanks. I've never…had my baking compared to sex before."

His cheek twitched, and she'd have sworn she heard a chuckle rumble from his chest.

"Well, I'm finished back here," Pete called to her as he shuffled out of the kitchen. "You'll lock up when you leave?"

Gage sent her a puzzled frown. "You're closing?" He flipped his wrist to check the large watch on his wide wrist. "It's only eight o'clock."

"This is a ranching town, Mr. Prescott. Most ranchers and their families have eaten dinner and headed to bed by now. Mornings come early in a ranch town, which means we're open at 4:00 a.m. to serve breakfast."

He lowered his brow and pressed his mouth in a firm line as if digesting this information.

"Well, then I should let you finish your work." He shoveled another couple of bites of pie in his mouth and gave her a nod as he rose from his stool.

"Don't rush off on my account. You can finish your pie, at least, then…maybe walk me to my car?"

He reached in his wallet and pulled out a couple of bills. "I'd be glad to walk you to your car, but…I wouldn't have thought a woman had to worry about being accosted in a small town like this."

Kate took off her apron and stashed it behind the counter. The infernal heat of her blush prickled her scalp again, as she gave him a bashful grin. "Well, yes…the town is quite safe, usually."

He tipped his head and arched an eyebrow. "Then…are you flirting with me, Miss Rogers?"

Her heart beat triple-time under his narrow-eyed scrutiny. "Well, if you have to ask, I'm obviously not doing it right."

He slid his check and payment across the counter to her. His expression lightened, and a small dimple appeared in his cheek. "On the contrary, I like your style."

Even that hint of a smile sent her pulse racing. And his dimple…dear Lord, that dimple softened the hard edge to him and made her weak in the knees.

Easy, girl. The man is only passing through town. Kate gathered her purse and pulled out her keys to lock up the diner, warning herself not to get any crazy ideas about Gage Prescott, security specialist. She might not know much about men, but she knew enough to be certain Gage was not the sort to settle down in a small town in the middle of Nowhere, Montana.

When Senator Kelley left town, so would his hunky body-guard.

As Gage drove back through the front gate of the Bar Lazy K, he found his mind drifting to Kate's sunny smile and her endearing tendency to blush at the slightest provocation. He gave his head a firm shake and redirected his thoughts to his client and the reasons he'd been hired.

He drove past the sprawling main house and pulled the truck up to the ranch hands' bunkhouse. In light of Kate's comment about ranchers heading to bed early, Gage found the amount of activity on the ranch intriguing. A large number of men still milled about outside the bunkhouse, including several men working near the stables. Gage knew almost nothing about ranching, but even to him this amount of activity after dark seemed unusual.

As he climbed out of the truck, the ranch manager, an older Native American man named Rusty Moore, approached him with a smile, three large dogs circling his legs, barking.

"Easy, Ace. He's a friend. Evening, Mr. Prescott. A successful trip?"

Gage tossed the keys back to Rusty. "Somewhat. Thanks again for the use of the truck."

"I'd say anytime, but the truth is this truck and most of the other vehicles will be tied up for the next several days. We leave early in the morning." Rusty reached down to give one of the dogs a good scratch behind the ear. "You'll guard the place while we're gone, won't ya, Ace? Good boy."

The dog's slow steps and gray muzzle told Gage the mutt was up in years, while the two others had the energy of youth. A black dog with a white spot on its head greeted Gage with a wiggle of excitement, planting his front paws on Gage's hip to nuzzle his hand.

"Domino! Get down!" Rusty fussed. "Sorry about that. Border collies are great for herding, but what they have in ranching skills, ours lack in manners."

Gage ruffled Domino's furry head. "I don't mind. I like dogs." He cast his gaze around the commotion and honed in on Rusty's earlier comment. "Why is everyone leaving tomorrow?"

The ranch manager nodded. "The annual roundup. We'll drive or ride into the hills and find all the cattle, load 'em up and bring them back to be sorted and sent to market. It's a big job so most everyone goes."

Gage rubbed his chin, deciding how the absence of all the ranch hands might affect his ability to protect the senator. Having the hands around was tantamount to having a fleet of guards watching for unusual activity on the property. In their absence, Gage and Bart would have a vast amount of land and several outbuildings to keep secure. "The stable and barn are monitored with security cameras, right?"

Rusty nodded. "All of the buildings are."

"But is anyone monitoring the camera feed or is the video only used to identify a trespasser when there's a problem?"

Rusty scoffed a laughed. "Mr. Cole doesn't have the manpower to have someone watching the camera feed around the clock. Problems are rare. Having this many hands around is security enough most days."

"Most days. But as you said, everyone is heading out tomorrow."

Rusty frowned. "Are you expecting a problem?"

Gage shrugged. "Hard to say. I wouldn't be here if trouble wasn't a possibility, and I wouldn't be doing my job if I didn't familiarize myself with all the security measures in place."

Rusty slid his fingers into the front pockets of his dusty jeans. "Cole should be up at the house by now. He can brief you on how the security system works."

Gage jerked a nod. "Thanks." He turned to head toward the main house then paused as Domino scampered across the yard in front of him. He shouldn't underestimate the value of the dogs as a warning system in the event of trespassers. "Mr. Moore?"

Rusty turned.

"What are the other dogs' names?"

The manager smiled and pointed to the older black dog with the gray muzzle. "That there is Ace. He's fifteen years young and the daddy of these other two. He sticks pretty close to home, seeing as how he's blind now." He pointed to the third dog, more white than the other two. "That's Mitzy, and you already met Domino. The younger two will go with us on roundup, so they won't be in your hair."

"I was actually thinking the dogs would help alert us in case of a break-in."

"Ordinarily they would, but we need 'em to work this week, herding cattle. But ol' Ace, even without his sight, he's still a pretty good guard dog. His hearing and sense of smell are still top-notch. He'll bark if he thinks there's a stranger we need to be alerted to."

Gage gave the old dog a considering scrutiny. "All right, Ace. You're my go-to guy out here. Got it?"

Hearing his name, Ace wobbled closer, tail wagging, and Gage let him sniff his hand before stroking the dog's head. Ace followed Gage as he crossed the dusty yard to the main house, a massive, multilevel home made of river rock and natural timber.

As he neared the main entrance, Cole's housekeeper, who'd been introduced to him earlier as Hannah Brown, appeared in the door. "There you are! I've had your dinner ready for an hour. Where have you been, mister?"

Gage blinked, startled by her scolding tone. He opened his mouth to tell the brusque older woman he'd eaten at Ira's Diner when he realized her gaze was on Ace rather than him.

"Come on, boy." She clicked her tongue and hitched her head toward the kitchen, confirming that her chastisements were for the dog. When she lifted her chin and directed an inquisitive look at Gage, he nodded a greeting. "Evening, Mr. Prescott. Can I get you anything from the kitchen before I head to bed?"

"No, ma'am. I've had dinner. If I need anything later, I'll get it for myself."

"No, you won't," she said, straightening her back and raising her head so that she appeared taller than her diminutive five-foot-two height. Her stern expression brooked no resistance. "There will be no rummaging about in my kitchen and leaving messes for me to find in the morning. If you want a drink, you can use Mr. Cole's wet bar in the family room. If you want to eat, get it now. After that, the kitchen is closed."

When they'd arrived earlier in the day, Senator Kelley had told him not to get on the housekeeper's bad side. "She's a piece of work that one. Been here since my father first built the ranch. She gave me my first spanking when I was four."

Gage inclined his head. "Roger that, ma'am. I won't disturb your kitchen."

She gave him a satisfied grin. "Good. I think we'll get along just fine." She tugged on the sleeve of her sweater as she headed to the kitchen with Ace at her feet. "Tell Hank breakfast is at five. I want Cole to have a good meal before he heads out. If Hank wants to take refuge here while his girlfriends are stirring up trouble, it's not my place to tell him no. But he can keep to the ranch's clock," she tossed over her shoulder in a clipped tone. "I won't be cooking two sets of meals every day just so he can keep a gentleman's schedule."

Gage gave a grunt of amusement. Cole Kelley's housekeeper reminded him of a few COs he'd had in recent years.

The sound of raised voices led Gage to the living room. Senator Kelley and his son stood on opposite sides of the room glaring at each other as they exchanged verbal volleys. Bart stood just behind the senator with his hands clasped behind his back.

"Do you ever think about anyone besides yourself?" Cole shouted at his father. "Are you really so stupid that you thought no one would find out?"

Gage hadn't yet been formally introduced to the ranch owner, but the resemblance to his twin brother made Cole's identity obvious.

"Watch your tone, Cole. I'm still a senator...and your father, and I deserve your respect."

Cole scoffed. "Respect has to be earned. And don't think I didn't notice that you mentioned being a senator before being my father. But then, that's how it's always been, hasn't it? So busy being Mr. Important that you put it before your family."

Gage drew a slow breath into tight lungs. Tension between the father and son made the air thick, suffocating.

"Maybe that used to be true, but—"

"I'm glad Mom left you." The son's tone was bitter. "It's about time. Frankly, I can't see why she stayed as long as she did."

Gage shifted his feet awkwardly, uncomfortable being a witness to the family argument. Judging by Bart's expression, he was of the same mind.

"It's a thing called loyalty, Cole," the senator returned. "But I wouldn't expect you to understand that."

"I give my loyalty where it's merited. When's the last time you gave me a reason to trust you?"

Henry Kelley's jaw tightened, but he made no reply.

Cole pulled an expression of exasperation and disgust. "I don't need this tonight." With a shake of his head, he turned to leave.

"Cole, wait!" The senator took a step, as if to pursue his son, but the rancher paused without facing his father.

"Something has happened that you should know about." Hank Kelley's voice rumbled low and unsteady.

Cole's shoulders drooped, and he rubbed his temple. "What, another of your bimbos crawl out from under a rock claiming to be carrying your child?"

"No, it's…worse." The senator sounded truly grieved, seriously upset.

Gage arched an eyebrow and perked his ears. When Dylan Kelley had hired him to guard the senator, he'd been vague about the situation, saying only that he feared his father was in danger and needed to lie low for a while. Gage had assumed his guard duty was directly related to Hank Kelley's numerous affairs, the women he'd betrayed, the constituents and backers he'd angered with his poor choices. But the gravity of his voice said there was much more at play.

Across the room, Cole huffed loudly, rolled his shoulders, and sent his father a dark glare. "To be honest, *Senator,*" he said, grating out the title like a foul word, "I'm about sick to death of hearing about the trouble your selfishness has caused our family. I have to leave the ranch before sunup tomorrow for the roundup. So, as much *fun* as this reunion has been, I'm done for tonight. You can dump your latest screwup on me when I get back next week."

With that, Cole stormed out.

The senator stared after his son with a forlorn expression, then cut an embarrassed glance to Gage. "I'm sorry about that. Obviously I'm not on the best of terms with my son. Haven't been for some time."

Gage cleared his throat and adjusted his stance. "With all due respect, sir, your personal business with your son only concerns me if he's a threat to your well-being. We've been hired to protect you, so if you think your son—"

"Good God, no! Cole might hate me—with good reason— but he's not out to hurt me! He's not part of—" The senator stopped abruptly, as if catching himself before he said too much.

Bart stepped forward, flanking the older man's other side. "Not part of what, sir?"

Hank shook his head and busied himself with collecting the newspaper spread on the chair beside him. "Never mind."

"Sir, if we are going to protect you, we need to know what we may be up against." Gage narrowed a hard look on the senator. "You need to tell us who and what threats have been made against you, what trouble you've had."

Hank dropped into the chair and closed his eyes. When he said nothing for several seconds, Bart prodded, "Sir?"

"It's…a private matter."

Bart shot Gage a look and rolled his eyes. While Gage shared the sentiment, he kept his mouth firmly set and his posture rigid. Professional. Detached. His job was to protect Senator Henry Kelley, not to like him. The senator, in fact, with his numerous affairs and blatant disregard for his family, confirmed Gage's belief that most people were rotten at the core. The best one could do in life was to guard your own interests and not grow too attached to anyone. That way, when inevitable disappointments came, the wounds didn't dig as deep.

Gage moved to the edge of the suede couch and sat across from the older man. "Senator, anything you tell us is strictly confidential. But you need to level with us if we are going to keep you safe."

Hank tapped a finger on the arm of the Western-style armchair and twisted his mouth. "Fine. Let's just say, I have…political enemies who…are pressuring me. I believe they could use physical threats to make their point and try to win my cooperation."

"Are these threats in relation to the women claiming to have had relationships with you?" Gage asked.

Hank's face reddened a shade, and he cut a side glance to Gage. "Not directly."

Gage suppressed the surge of impatience that spiked his pulse when the senator continued to equivocate. The man's flushed skin told Gage he was lying but also called to mind Kate Rogers's tendency to blush. What had been sexy and intriguing on the pretty waitress was an irritating sign of noncooperation with the senator.

Leaning toward the senator, Gage flipped up his palm in inquiry. "Can you be more specific?"

Hank sighed. "Look, Gage, I know you're just trying to do your job, but…I didn't hire you. Dylan did. I'm not happy with the idea of being here. It smacks of hiding from the press and the women who've come forward. I hate looking like a coward. I have important matters to tend to—both personal and business—but for reasons I don't care to elaborate on, I'm here. Do your babysitting thing, if you must—"

Gage ground his back teeth at the man's derogatory characterization of his job.

"—since that's what you're being paid to do, but I'd prefer to keep my private concerns private. No offense intended."

Hank raised a highball glass to lips, and while the senator drank, Gage met Bart's eyes. The subtle flicker of impatience and disgust in his colleague's expression mirrored the frustration bubbling inside Gage—a feeling he determinedly quashed. Emotions had no place in his line of work. He simply needed to do his job.

As Gage shoved to his feet, ready to leave the protection of the senator in Bart's hands until his shift started in the morning, Hank released a weary sigh and muttered, "They kidnapped my daughter."

Gage hesitated, not certain he'd heard correctly, then lowered himself back onto the suede couch. "Excuse me?"

Bart circled the chair where the senator sat and settled next to Gage.

"My daughter, Lana, was kidnapped a couple of days ago." His tone was hushed, defeated. "Her kidnappers called me and made it clear her release was contingent upon my cooperation with their demands." A muscle in his jaw twitched. "I'm being blackmailed."

Gage battled down the kick in his pulse. Now they were getting somewhere. "Have you notified the authorities?"

The senator's gaze darted up to his. "No. And neither can you. I was warned not to contact the police or the FBI if I wanted Lana to live."

"A common enough threat, but the FBI needs to—"

"No!" The senator's eyes flashed. "This is my problem, and we do things my way. Period. It's imperative that I not give these people reason to retaliate."

"What people?" Bart asked.

Hank's Adam's apple bobbed as he swallowed. "I...can't tell you. It's complicated."

"If your daughter's life is at stake—"

"I have my own resources. I'm looking into ways to facilitate a rescue but...I need time to plan. I'm still trying to determine where they're holding her."

Gage flopped back on the couch, staring at the senator, trying to keep the sour words that sprang to his tongue in check. He thought of Cole's parting shot about what the senator's selfishness had cost his family and understood better the depth of the son's animosity.

Now Hank Kelley, U.S. Senator from California, was jeopardizing his daughter's life in order to cover his political ass. Or at least that's how it appeared. Whatever dirt his enemies had to blackmail him with couldn't be as important as saving his daughter from her kidnappers. Yet to appease his enemies, Hank refused to contact the FBI. Gage's low opinion of the senator dropped another notch.

"Sir, while I don't know all the particulars of the situation," Bart said, "I'd be remiss if I didn't encourage you to contact the authorities immediately and tell them everything you can about the kidnap—"

"I said *no*," Hank growled. "Case closed. I'll handle this my way." The senator slammed down his glass and shot to his feet. "I'm going to bed. I'm not to be disturbed before 8:00 a.m."

Bart stood quickly and followed their charge.

Gage opened his mouth to tell the senator what the housekeeper had said about the 5:00 a.m. breakfast but decided not to waste his breath. If the senator missed his last chance to speak to his son before Cole headed out for roundup, it was none of his business. Family matters were a distraction Gage didn't want to involve himself in. His job was to keep the senator safe, and that was what Gage intended to do.

* * *

Broken bodies littered the earth. Blood ran through the dust in tiny rivers. Moans of the dying assailed his ears. Gage staggered through the wreckage of Humvees and dead soldiers. Disoriented. Confused. Grieving. Where had the attack come from? The road had been clear and then…

He spotted Mike, his best friend in the unit, staring sightlessly into the gray day. And there was Gunner. So young. So cocky. So dead. Further down the convoy, his CO lay with his arms still clutching the wound in his gut. Dead. They were all dead.

A sob lurched from Gage's chest. Dark despair. Loss. Guilt.

The road had looked clear. He'd told them to proceed. Sweat mingled with his tears as he stumbled down the rutted road. The eyes of his dead unit followed him. The hands of slaughtered soldiers reached out to grab his ankles. *Murderer. You failed us.*

The breath in his lungs weighted him down like the cold boulders lining the road. He wheezed, choked on the fumes of leaking fuel.

Darrius. Frank. Jimmy B. His head spun as one face followed another. Gone. Bloodied. Broken. Walt. Mad Dog. Ronnie. And…

He froze. His gaze fell on the new face.

Blood streaked her creamy skin. Dust dimmed her golden highlights. Death stole her sunny smile. *Kate.*

Gage jerked awake, gasping. Sweat bathed his skin, and horror knotted his gut. His gaze darted around the unfamiliar dark room, searching…

No dead soldiers. No dusty road. No Kate.

Nightmare. Again. He muttered a foul curse. Curling his fingers into his sheets, he fought to gain control over his ragged breathing. The rapid-fire beat of his heart.

His bedding had twisted around his legs as he thrashed.

With jerky tugs, he freed his feet and swung them to the floor. He lifted his watch from the bedside table and checked the time. Oh three hundred. He had to be up in three hours, ready to guard a selfish senator whose enemies had kidnapped his daughter. A cushy assignment compared to being deployed in Afghanistan.

Gage gritted his teeth. He didn't deserve cushy. He deserved to have been brought home in a casket like his friends. Protecting the convoy had been his job, and he'd let his unit down.

Why had God spared him? Maybe the nightmares were his punishment. An ongoing reminder of his failure. As if he'd ever forget.

Gage choked back the fist of grief that rose in his throat with the bitter taste of bile.

The dream had changed tonight. What did it mean that Kate was now among the dead?

Why, sir, are you flirting with me?

Gage shuddered and tried to block the image of her lifeless, bloody face. Kate had no place in his nightmare. But maybe that was the point—a stark reminder that he was damaged. That his world was no place for Kate, with her sunshine laugh and blushing innocence. He was only passing through town. As soon as the senator moved on, so would Gage.

Kate might be a breath of fresh air in the dank cave of his life, but he had no room for distraction. And she didn't need his black cloud obliterating her light.

Chapter 3

"Get down, you mongrel!" Hank snarled when Ace greeted the senator by planting his muddy paws on the man's Italian suit.

Gage stepped forward and whistled for the border collie. "Ace. Here, boy."

Obediently, Ace walked slowly over, wagging his tail, and Gage scratched the elderly dog's head. Across the yard, the outbuildings seemed eerily quiet compared to the activity just last night. A dry wind blew the scent of manure up from the stables, and Gage could almost imagine a tumbleweed rolling through the deserted ranch. Poor dog was probably lonely, what with everyone, including the other dogs, gone on roundup.

"Stupid dog," Hank grumbled, swiping mud from his pants.

Grouch, Gage thought, opening the back door of the Lincoln Town Car for the senator. What kind of man doesn't like dogs?

Already, after barely twenty-four hours in Montana, Hank had grown tired of sitting around the ranch's main house and decided to get lunch in town—contrary to Gage's advice to stay put and keep a low profile.

"That's why I have you for protection," Hank had countered. "So I can go places and do things with you to watch my back."

So they were headed into Maple Cove for lunch at Ira's Diner, and Gage was trying not to think about seeing Kate again. His stomach knotted when he remembered her face as it had appeared in his nightmare. Still. Blood-streaked. Lifeless.

"From now on, when we go anywhere, you keep that mutt away from me." Hank frowned at Gage before he climbed into the back seat. "I don't need any more suits ruined."

"Yes, sir." Gage gave Ace another furtive pat before sliding behind the steering wheel. *Good dog.*

Hannah Brown appeared at the back door and called to Ace. The dog's ears perked, and he trotted off, following the sound of her voice.

Gage drove north into Maple Cove, listening to the senator grumble in the back seat about the spotty cell phone reception for his BlackBerry. When they reached the small town, Gage parked in front of Ira's Diner, and anticipation jangled his nerves as though he were a grunt on his first day of basic training. *Get a grip, soldier.*

"Nothing's changed." The senator's voice dripped with condescension. "I've been gone more than thirty years, but nothing ever changes in the booming metropolis of Maple Cove, Montana."

"We could always go back to the ranch," Gage suggested. *Coward.*

"No. Let's go." The senator opened his door and climbed

out before Gage could reply. Before he could do a visual sweep of the street for any potential threats.

Gage scowled. "If I'm going to do my job, Senator Kelley, I need you to follow my directions without question. If I say jump, you're to jump immediately. No questions asked. Understand?"

The senator shot him a dirty look as he headed into the diner. "Not even to ask how high?"

Gage paused on the sidewalk and braced his hands at his waist, glaring at the senator. A cool October wind, laced with tantalizing scents from the diner, ruffled his hair and stung his cheeks. "A sniper's rifle can fire a bullet at upwards of three thousand feet per second. If you took the time to question my order, you'd be dead before the words left your mouth."

Hank hiked up his chin, but his face paled. "No need to get testy."

"I just want us to be clear. I can't protect you if you don't follow my directives."

His expression contrite, Hank turned to gaze down the street. "Fine. But I'm used to giving orders, not taking them."

"Understood. And I respect the authority of your office. But Bart and I need your full cooperation to keep you safe."

Hank straightened his tie and nodded tightly. "Got it." He turned on his heel and marched into the diner, leaving Gage to follow.

"Rule one," Gage mumbled, repeating the terms he and Bart had laid out days ago when they'd first taken the assignment of protecting Senator Kelley, "I enter a building first."

Stepping into the diner, Gage hesitated by the door, letting his eyes adjust to the dimmer light and sweeping an encompassing gaze around the room. He was *not* looking for Kate, he told himself. Just getting a feel for the lunch crowd and the mood of the room as the newly notorious senator from California entered the diner.

Heads swivelled to stare. Conversations died. A murmur flowed around them as recognition dawned on the other patrons.

When an older woman with her hands full with takeout boxes approached the exit, Gage opened the door and held it while the lady toddled out.

"Hello, Senator Kelley," a bright voice said. "Welcome to Ira's."

Gage's heart missed a beat as he turned to find Kate setting out clean utensils at the table behind them.

She flashed the senator a bright smile before aiming the full wattage on Gage.

Steady, boy.

"Back so soon, Gage? You did like my pie, then, didn't you?" She added a wink, and Gage's breath stuck in his chest. God, she was even prettier than he'd remembered. Today she wore her wheat-blond hair pinned back with barrettes shaped like butterflies, giving him an unimpeded view of the sparkle in her blue eyes.

He clenched his teeth long enough to catch his breath and form a reply that didn't sound like the babbling of a lovestruck sap. "The senator had cabin fever."

The teasing light in her face dimmed slightly, as if his response disappointed her. Mentally he kicked himself. *Yes, Miss Rogers, I enjoyed your pie a lot. I'm looking forward to another slice for dessert.* Yeah, that might have been more what she was looking for.

Gage scowled, frustrated with his schoolboy jitters and took a seat at the table next to Senator Kelley.

Kate handed them each a menu as another waitress brought glasses of ice water to them. "This is Ms. Emerson. She'll be your server today."

"Howdy, folks," the brunette with sprinkles of gray at her temples and a pencil stuck over her ear said. "Our special today is roasted chicken and rice."

Kate walked back to the counter as the waitress, whose name tag read Laurie, recited the soups of the day. Gage listened with only half interest, while another glance around the restaurant located Janet. Even from this distance, Gage could see the bruises on Janet's arm and the shadow of a black eye under her makeup.

Fury roiled in his blood toward the man who'd inflicted the wounds. He could only imagine how frustrated Kate must be trying to free her sister from the abusive marriage.

"What'll you have, honey?"

Called from his musings by Laurie Emerson's question, Gage jerked his attention back to his table. "The special is fine."

"Good choice." Laurie winked, then cast her gaze in the direction he'd been staring. "Sorry, partner, Janet, over there, is married. Don't get any ideas."

Gage opened his mouth to deny Laurie's assumption, but she swished away with their order before he could speak. He shot a look at Hank, who was busy scoping out the other diners and the Western-themed decor of the small-town establishment. Gage took the opportunity to study Kate, who laughed as she talked to an older gentleman seated on a stool at the long lunch counter. She opened the pastry cooler and removed a pie with a fluffy meringue, and her customer patted his heart and nodded.

"I'll have some of that if you're serving, Kate," another man called across the diner.

"Hold your horses, Gene!" she called back with a beatific grin. "There's plenty!"

And so it went for the next several minutes as Gage and Hank ate their lunch, exchanging only occasional small talk.

Kate chatted amiably with the ranchers and other townsfolk, serving up cake, pie and other pastries with an unfailing smile. Every few minutes, she would glance in his direction, and Gage made no secret of the fact that he was watching. He'd nod or raise his eyebrows in acknowledgment, and Kate would flash a quick grin and flush to her roots, then busy herself with some trivial task.

Meanwhile, Janet, between serving bowls of chili and stew, cast her sister hooded glares. When Kate would get especially chatty with one of the younger men lunching at the counter, Janet invariably stalked over with some terse comment that would send Kate off to the kitchen or another customer.

Gage folded his arms over his chest and pondered his observations. Janet seemed unwilling to let her sister enjoy the easy rapport she had with the customers. She seemed...*jealous* of the attention, the compliments and the laughter Kate received. Especially from men.

When Hank answered a call on his BlackBerry, Gage faced the senator with a curious lift of his brow.

The senator blanched, clearly rattled by whoever was on the phone. "Oh my God! Where are you?" he gasped, then rose quickly and carried the phone to a far corner of the diner, plugging one ear with a finger.

Gage stood, as well, prepared to follow the senator if he left the room. As long as he stayed in sight, Gage allowed Hank privacy for his call. With his attention riveted on his client, he didn't see Kate approach his table with a white pastry box in her hands.

Kate tried to squash the girlish flutter in her stomach as she set the box on the table and tapped Gage on the shoulder. He turned with a startled jerk and a frown. His stern expression almost deterred her from pursuing any conversation with him. Didn't the man ever smile? But she recalled how he'd held the door for Mrs. Bradshaw earlier and, coupled with his willingness to defend her and Janet against Larry the night before, that simple courtesy gave her hope that a good-hearted and gallant man resided beneath his dour yet handsome facade.

"These are for you." She nodded toward the box. "To say thank you for stepping in last night to help out with Larry. Not many men in this town are willing to tangle with my brother-in-law."

Gage glanced at the box, then redirected his penetrating gaze on her. Those cool, deep blue eyes had followed her movements around the diner since he'd arrived, and she'd felt the weight of his stare like a physical touch. Intimate and personal. Distracting.

She worked to hide the nervous twitch in her grin as she laid a hand on the box. "They're eclairs. Chocolate. I made them this morning. For you."

Dear heavens, under his unnerving stare she couldn't even form a whole sentence. She sounded like a babbling idiot!

He covered her hand with his, scooting hers aside so he could lift the box lid. "You made these?"

She shrugged. "No big deal. I was already doing the day's baking and...well, I just wanted to thank you. You do like chocolate, don't you?"

He nodded once. "Thanks."

Abruptly, Gage's attention darted across the room to the senator, who was still deep in conversation on his cell phone.

Had she imagined the chemistry she'd experienced with him last night? He seemed distant today, despite his piercing gaze. "Well...enjoy them," she mumbled awkwardly. "And thanks again."

"Kate."

She faced him again, her heart tapping with a schoolgirl's hope and anticipation. "Yeah?"

"Does Janet always act that way toward you?"

She gave him a puzzled frown. "Act what way?"

Before he could answer, Charlie Stokes drove past the diner, his ancient truck backfiring with a loud *boom*.

Instantly, Gage dropped low behind the table, jerking her to the floor beside him.

"Get down!" he roared, sending a wave of panic and series of gasps through the diner. Especially when he dug a large handgun from under his jacket and scrambled in a crouch to the corner of the diner where Hank Kelley huddled behind a stack of extra chairs.

Kate clapped a hand to her chest and chuckled a nervous laugh. "Easy, cowboy. Put away the weapon. That was just Mr. Stokes's 1957 pickup backfiring."

Slowly the other diners realized Gage's alarm had been for naught and returned to their meals with shakes of their heads. Kate scurried across the room, a reassuring hand raised toward Gage.

The senator and Gage cast another look around the room for good measure, then Gage put a hand under Hank Kelley's elbow to help him back to his feet. "Right." He clamped his lips in a scowl. "Still, I couldn't take the chance that it wasn't a truck. I—" He released a deep breath that shuddered out of him. "Are you all right, Senator?"

Hank nodded, frowning at his bodyguard. "Fine, but…I'm ready to go. I—" he cleared his throat and dusted invisible dirt from his suit-coat sleeve "—have business to take care of."

Hank walked to the register in clipped strides, fishing out his wallet to settle the bill.

But Gage didn't follow. Instead, he braced a hand against the back wall and stared blankly at the floor while sweat beaded on his brow. He sawed out ragged breaths, and the muscles in his arms trembled.

Concern jabbed Kate, and she stepped closer, placing a hand on his broad back. "Gage, are you all right?"

His head snapped up, and his eyes flickered with a wild light. Blinking hard, he took a couple of deep gulps of air and tucked the gun at the small of his back again.

"I—I'm fine. I just—" Sucking in a big breath that flared his nostrils, he shoved away from the wall and squared his shoulders. For the first time since she'd met him, he refused to meet her gaze. "Thank you again…for the pastries."

Without further explanation, he marched past her, took the box of eclairs from their table and escorted the senator out of the diner.

Kate stared after him, bewildered. What had caused such a drastic reaction from him? The stone-faced tough guy she'd met last night had…*cracked.* But what did she really know about him? Judging by his defense of Janet last night and the way he'd pulled her out of harm's way a few minutes ago when he'd thought there was danger, Kate guessed protective-ness was more than an occupation for him. Gage held doors for ladies and had the presence of mind to thank her for the eclairs, even when he'd clearly been rattled by the backfiring truck. Gallant and well-mannered. A modern-day knight.

Kate smiled to herself as she returned to work. If she were a damsel in distress, she could do a lot worse than to have hunky, brooding Gage Prescott coming to her rescue.

"From now on," Gage said as he backed the Town Car out onto the main street of Maple Cove, "I'm no more than three feet from you anytime we are in public. Got it?"

"That was a private phone call."

Gage shrugged. "I'm discreet. I won't disclose any of your personal business, nor will I intentionally eavesdrop."

Hank grunted. "I've heard that before."

"My only interest is in being close enough to you that I

can protect you from a sniper or kidnapper. I was wrong to let you leave the table without me. I won't repeat that mistake."

Gage wished he had a do-over on the last ten minutes for personal reasons, too. He hated the thought that Kate had seen his reaction to the truck backfiring.

A freaking truck *backfiring.* And he'd gone ballistic. Damn it, he'd heard enough gunfire in his life to know the difference between a sniper rifle and a truck backfiring. And yet he'd had a little meltdown. Right there in front of Kate, the senator and half the town of Maple Cove. Gage squeezed the steering wheel and sighed his disgust. One *boom,* and he was right back on that infernal Afghan road, shaking like a sissy and sweating like a whore. He clenched his teeth. What must Kate think?

Hank grumbled something that sounded like "damn babysitter," then sighed as his cell rang again. "Yes?" he answered in a clipped tone.

Gage glanced in the rearview mirror at the senator as he took the call. Hank stiffened, and his face paled. "Who is this? Where is Lana?"

Lana. A chill spun through Gage. The senator's kidnapped daughter.

"I'm clear on your demands, but—" Hank's voice held an undeniable wobble.

Pulling the car to a stop at the side of the country road, Gage pivoted to face the senator in the backseat, listening and watching intently. Hank met his gaze, the fear in his eyes unmistakable.

"I want to talk to Lana. I want proof that she is alive and well!" the senator barked. When his expression shifted, softened, Gage knew the kidnappers had complied. "Lana! How are you? *Where* are you?" Hank listened intently, his eyes filling with moisture. He nodded, swallowed hard. "Same here, darling. I— Lana?" Again Hank's face tightened. "Listen here, you cretin, if you hurt her, I'll—" He jerked. "Hello? Hello? Damn it!" The senator jabbed his disconnect button, scowling.

Gage gave Hank only a moment to collect himself. "What did your daughter say? Did she give you any useful information?"

The senator glanced up, frowning, clearly ready to tell Gage to mind his own business. But he hesitated, then shook his head. "No. She just had a personal message for me." He furrowed his brow, mumbling, "An oddly worded one at that."

"Oddly worded…how?" Gage pressed. "Tell me exactly what she said. What noises could you hear in the background?"

Hank pressed his mouth in a stubborn line. "My relationship with my daughter is none of your business."

Gage narrowed an equally mulish glare on the senator. "It is if her kidnapping, the people holding her, the threats and demands her kidnappers have made affect my ability to keep you safe. I need to know everything about that call and any others you receive from the blackmailers. Tell me what she said, what the kidnapper said. Verbatim."

Hank turned toward the window, folding his arms over his chest. For a moment, he said nothing, his turbulent thoughts and emotions playing across his creased face. "The man said the same thing they've always said—that if I want Lana returned, I know what I have to do."

"Which is?" Gage prompted.

Hank jerked his attention back to Gage, his jaw rigid. "Non-negotiable and top secret."

Gage clenched his teeth. How was he supposed to protect the senator when the man wouldn't tell him what or who they were up against?

Hank shifted on the seat and cleared his throat. "Then

Lana said, and I quote, 'On the remote chance that I survive this ordeal, I hope we can elevate our relationship to a higher place.' Period. Then they took the phone away from her, repeated their warning and hung up."

Gage repeated Lana's statement, puzzling over the awkward phrasing. Was her wording choice a matter of nerves or was she telling her father something?

Hank dragged a hand over his mouth and sighed wearily. "As you saw last night with Cole, I haven't been an especially good father in recent years. I traveled a lot on business, worked late, gave my career priority over family more often than not." Hank cast Gage a brief guilty glance before turning toward the window again. "Cole resents me, especially now, with all my…indiscretions coming to light." Another sigh. "Can't say that I blame him."

Gage arched an eyebrow. That admission, for a senator who'd been as self-involved as Hank Kelley, was rather significant. Too bad Cole wasn't here to hear it.

Gage hadn't been close to his own father, but at least no animosity lingered between them the way Cole resented the senator.

"But Lana was different," the senator said, pulling Gage out of his musings. "Lana always stood by me, gave me the benefit of the doubt. So for her to say we need to work on our relationship—"

"Elevate," Gage corrected as he pulled the Town Car back onto the road.

"What?"

"You quoted her as saying she hoped you could *elevate* your relationship. I think her word choice was intentional."

"Are you saying she was sending me a cryptic message?" Skepticism darkened Hank's tone.

Gage shrugged. "Possible. Can you think of another reason for her odd phrasing?"

"I— No. What do you think she was saying?"

"Good question." Gage chewed the inside of his cheek as he drove past the endless stretch of pasture land, the jagged silhouette of the nearby mountains looming before them. "Elevate could mean elevators. That and the bit about a higher place... Maybe she was saying something about a high-rise building...somewhere you'd have to take an elevator to the top floor."

"A tall building, hmm?" Hank scoffed. "Well, that narrows it down, doesn't it?"

Gage cast Hank a withering glance in the rearview mirror. "We're brainstorming here, talking through the possibilities." *Jerk.*

"Fine. So my highly educated daughter was telling me, not that she hoped to have a closer relationship with me but that she was being held in a tall building with an elevator," Hank groused. "Brilliant."

"Actually, I think any clue she could pass to you without tipping her hand to her kidnappers is very crafty." Gage rolled the ache in his shoulders. When he'd dived for the floor at the diner, he'd caught the edge of the table. His arm would be sporting a good bruise tonight. "Give her credit."

"Oh, I do. But your interpretations of her clues are rather thin, don't you think?"

They'd reached the entrance to the Bar Lazy K Ranch, and Gage drove through the raw timber arch. "*Elevate* could refer to professional rank or position. Although she said higher place. That makes me think she's talking about a location." Gage glanced in the rearview mirror again to assess the senator's reaction to this hypothesis. And the reflection of the Absaroka Mountains behind them caught his attention.

"Elevate...elevation...higher place..." One thought tumbled onto the next as certainty swelled in him. Gage braked hard and swivelled to stare through the back window. "Maybe she was saying she's in the mountains. She could even be in those mountains." He aimed a finger at the range on the horizon.

Hank tensed and turned to look out at the rugged peaks. "My family has owned property in or near Maple Cove for three generations. That's public knowledge." A muscle in Hank's jaw twitched. "She was taken in Europe, but…it's certainly possible the kidnappers would hold her near here."

Gage drummed the steering wheel with his fingers as he started the car inching up the gravel road to the main house. "It's one possibility, but we can't fixate on one idea to the exclusion of others."

He knew better than to expect the senator to give him any credit for having worked through Lana's puzzle even that far. Gage schooled his expression and parked on the drive in front of the main house.

"Once we figure out where she is, I can finally do something to help her." Hank's tone rang with an optimism that bothered Gage.

"Meaning you'll call the FBI?"

"No. The kidnappers were clear. No police." Hank sliced the air with his hand. "I'll only call the FBI as a last resort."

Gritting his teeth to bite back his opinion of Hank's stubbornness, Gage climbed out of the car and scanned the property for threats with a careful eye. From the door by the kitchen, Ace trotted up, tongue lolling, to greet the arriving guests, and Gage held the dog's collar while Hank got out of the car.

"Sir, I understand your reluctance to defy the people holding your daughter, but the FBI—"

"No FBI!" Hank growled and straightened his sleeves. "I have my own resources and personal reasons not to involve the authorities. When the time is right, I'll have Lana rescued on my own terms." Turning on his heel, the senator marched toward the house, his chin high.

Gage closed the car door and used the key fob to lock the doors as he followed the senator inside. He could only hope Senator Kelley's selfish agenda didn't get his daughter killed.

Chapter 4

The eclairs were to die for.

Gage chewed the first sweet bite, letting the chocolate-cream filling and flaky pastry melt against his tongue, and he couldn't help but groan in ecstasy. He'd never tasted anything so delicious. Not counting the apple pie he'd had when he'd stopped by the diner for supper his first night in town.

He took another bite and propped his feet up on the bed in his guest room, settling in for a quiet evening with the television and a dessert box full of indulgence. No doubt about it, Kate could bake like a champion.

Gage dipped his finger into the middle of the eclair and dug out a scoop of the chocolate filling. He stared at the sweet treat he'd excavated and imagined using the cream filling to paint his initials on a certain wheat-blond pastry chef's naked belly. Closing his eyes, he pictured himself licking the chocolate from her skin, sucking it from her fingers and smearing it on her—

Wrroooopp.

The whoop of an alarm shattered the calm of the night, and Gage lunged to his feet. Adrenaline pumped through him, kicking his heartbeat into overdrive as he hurried toward the senator's suite.

He met Bart and the senator in the hall as the night-duty bodyguard hustled Hank toward the wine-cellar-cum-panic room.

"Any idea what triggered the alarm?" Gage asked Bart as he fell in step beside them, one hand on his service weapon.

Bart shook his head. "None. Once I get the senator to the wine cellar, I'll check the monitors in the security office."

"No, you stay with him until the all-clear." He nodded toward Hank, who frowned back. "I'll check the monitors and the property."

"For crying out loud, I'm not a child!" the senator grumbled to Bart. "You don't have to sit with me while he does all the work."

Bart leaned closer to Gage, muttering over the shriek of the alarm. "I'm thinking you have the easy assignment this go-around."

Hannah appeared at the end of the hall, waving them toward a stairwell near the kitchen. "This way, Senator."

Gage saw Hank, Bart, Hannah and an orange cat the housekeeper clutched in her arms down the steps to the security of the reinforced wine cellar, then headed to the first-floor room where the security system's master controls were set up. He surveyed the bank of monitors, checking each screen for unusual activity.

Problem was, he knew too little about ranch life to know what was normal and what might be suspicious. A man in a cowboy hat was in the stables, apparently calming a horse that had been spooked by the sirens at the main house. The ranch hands' bunkhouse was eerily dark and still in the absence of the men who'd left that morning on roundup.

When the phone in the security office rang, Gage answered the call.

"This is Cole. Who am I talking to?"

"Gage Prescott. From your father's security team."

"I had a call from the sheriff that the security alarm at the ranch had gone off. Is...my father all right?"

Gage heard genuine concern in Cole's voice. Despite the hard feelings and distance between the rancher and his father, Gage sensed a family affection that said all was not lost for that relationship.

"We have your father in the secure room. I'm checking the monitors now but don't see anything out of the ordinary. I can call you back once I go outside to check the property."

"Nah. Wes will call me if there's anything to report."

"Wes?"

"Wes Colton, the county sheriff. He's on his way to check things out, give you backup."

"Got it." Gage thought about telling Cole about the phone call Hank had received today from the kidnappers, but he'd sworn his discretion to the senator and refused to break that vow. After assuring Cole that everything was under control at the ranch and he didn't need to return from the roundup early, Gage found a flashlight and pulled his jacket from the front closet before heading out into the chilly October night.

A curtain of fog swirled through the dark evening, giving the moonlight a muted glow.

Gage had just finished a preliminary search of the perimeter of the main house when a set of headlights pierced the night, traveling up the long gravel drive from the highway.

Gage strode out to meet the arriving car and offered his hand to the uniformed man who stepped out of the patrol car.

After exchanging introductions with the sheriff, Gage and

Wes began a thorough search of the grounds. A more careful inspection of the main house yielded nothing, as did the check of the barn, but at the empty bunkhouse, Gage found a broken window on the back wall. "Sheriff, take a look."

As Wes approached, Gage shone his flashlight on the ground below the window and spotted a set of foot impressions in the dusty dirt.

"What have you got?" Wes asked.

"This doesn't look like a simple accident to me." Gage pointed out the footprints and shattered glass, then aimed his flashlight through the window to the bunkhouse floor where a brick lay in the middle of the floor.

The pale moonlight cast harsh shadows across the sheriff's chiseled face, and a muscle jumped in his jaw. "Could be simple vandalism, but…this does seem fishy to me. Anyone who lives around here knows the hands are out on roundup, and nobody is home at the bunkhouse. So why target the bunkhouse?"

Gage rubbed the back of his neck. "Good question."

"I'll get a team out here to get a mold of this footprint and see if we can lift any prints from the brick."

Gage gave a tight nod. "I'll keep looking, maybe see if I can tell which way the vandal left the area."

The sheriff promised to call Cole and inform him of the damaged window, and Gage continued a sweep of the property. He found little else to indicate who might have broken the window or why. At the stable, he found the man he'd seen on the security monitor, still with the same restless horse. After introducing himself, Gage asked if the hand, who said his name was Ben Radley, had seen or heard anything just before the alarm went off.

Ben shook his head. "I've been busy all night with Blaze here. He's got colic, and all my attention has been on him."

As far as Gage knew, colic was something that made

babies cranky, but he didn't bother to ask why the horse's case needed full-time care.

"That alarm sure did startle us, though. What's all the ruckus?" the ranch hand asked.

Gage explained about the broken window, then asked, "So why didn't you go with the others on the roundup?"

"Cole asked me to stay and take care of things here." Ben stroked the horse's nose. "Good thing, too, with Blaze showin' up with colic."

Gage glanced down the stall and noticed a couple of other horses and a fat black cat curled up at the other end of the building.

"Why didn't they take those other horses with them on roundup?" he asked.

Ben shrugged. "Well, Hermes has a lame foot, and Spike over there is too young to work still." The ranch hand tapped his cowboy hat back and grinned. "Besides, nowadays ranchers use trucks and four-wheelers and so forth as often as not."

Blaze gave a loud whinny and tried to lie down, but Ben yanked up on the horse's bridle and forcibly kept the horse on his feet. "Oh, no you don't, buddy. Stay up."

Seeing the man had his hands full, Gage asked Ben to keep an eye out for any unusual activity and left him to his task with the sick horse.

When he reached the main house, he headed back to the security office and radioed Bart in the wine cellar. "All clear."

"Roger that," the other bodyguard's voice crackled over the walkie-talkie.

When the senator, Bart and the housekeeper emerged from the basement, Gage filled them in on what he and the sheriff had found.

"Well, Pumpkin and I have had all the excitement we want for one day. Good night, all," Hannah said as she carried the big orange cat off to the back of the house.

Hank, too, wasted no time heading back to his guest suite, and Bart and Gage escorted him down the hall. In light of the breach of the alarm system, Gage performed a quick search of the senator's bedroom and bath before allowing the man back inside. The senator's cell phone rang as Gage cleared him to enter the suite, and Gage wondered who would be calling at this late hour.

Hank answered the cell, and his face hardened when the caller spoke.

"What do you want?" Hank's icy tone caught Gage's attention as he was leaving for his own guest room.

Gage exchanged a look with Bart. Could the call have repercussions for the senator's safety? A clue as to who had broken the window at the bunkhouse?

And where was the charming and charismatic man who'd been reelected to the U.S. senate five times? Gage knew the man was under stress, having his daughter kidnapped and his own life threatened, but he had yet to see much evidence of the suave, gentleman senator that the media had portrayed for years.

"After the way you sold me out to the press? You've got to be kidding!" Hank scoffed. "My wife left me, you know."

The senator tunneled fingers through his hair and dropped onto the edge of his bed. "Forget it. It's too late for that."

Color suffused Hank's face, and Bart sent Gage another curious look.

"No." The senator sighed heavily. "Don't cry. I hate that. And I won't let you blackmail me with these veiled threats."

Gage checked his watch. His shift officially started in five hours, and he wanted to catch some *z's* before then. But if the senator's call was half as dramatic as it sounded, the caller could be a danger to the senator.

"No. It's over, Gloria. Even if I wanted to pick up where

we ended things, don't you think the press is watching me like a hawk? No, I can't meet you. I'm not in town."

Gage tensed. Crap. Who was the senator talking to? He'd just spilled a key bit of information that could compromise his safety. He gave the senator a stern glare, signaling him to hang up, but Hank only turned his back to Gage.

"No, Gloria. I'm sorry. I can't. I've got too much heat on me as it is. Don't call again." Finally, Hank disconnected and faced his bodyguards' unhappy stares.

"You told her you weren't in town," Bart grated in an even tone before Gage could. "Have you listened to anything we've said? What good does it do to tuck you away up here in Podunk, Montana, if you tell everyone where you are?"

Hank squared his shoulders. "I didn't tell her where I was. Only that I wasn't at home."

"So who was that? What was it about?" Gage asked.

Hank glared at Gage. "It was private business."

"Senator, you have no private business until this threat against you has been resolved," Bart said.

Senator Kelley huffed loudly. "Fine. Her name is Gloria Cosgrove and…she's one of the women I had a thing with recently. She wants to see me. Wants to get back together. I said no. She got weepy and begged for a meet. I told her it was over and not to call again." The senator pulled a face that said, *There. Are you happy now?* "But then you heard all that, didn't you?"

Gloria Cosgrove. Gage made a mental note to check the woman out.

"Just be careful. The less people know about you, the safer you are," Bart said.

The senator scowled and stalked toward the bottle of Maker's Mark on the desk.

"I'll be in my room," Gage told Bart as he left the senator's suite, his neck tense and his jaw aching from clenching his teeth.

Bart followed him into the hall. "You know, I was thinking about that security alarm tonight. What if it was a test?"

Gage frowned. "What kind of test?"

"What if whoever triggered the alarm was watching our response?"

Gage mulled the idea, a sharp gnawing in his gut. "You mean, looking for weaknesses in the system?"

"Right. A dry run as it were."

The idea sent a prickle down the back of Gage's neck. "Certainly a possibility we can't ignore."

"What's your gut telling you about this woman that just called? Problem for us?"

Gage shrugged. "A woman scorned is always gonna be an unknown we need to consider. But is she part of the bigger picture, the kidnapping of the senator's daughter?" Gage rolled his hand up.

Bart twisted his mouth. "Yeah. Seems unlikely." He glanced back toward the bedroom where the senator was settling back in the king-size bed. "Well, 'night."

"G'night." Gage ducked into the guest room across the hall from Hank's and cast a longing glance to the box of eclairs he'd abandoned when the alarm sounded. As tasty as the pastries were, he'd lost his appetite while dealing with the smug and resentful senator. He stashed the box on a shelf in his closet and toed off his shoes.

Maybe if he revisited his fantasy about licking the chocolate-cream filling off Kate's skin, he could hold his nightmares at bay tonight.

Kate pulled a loaf of banana bread out of the oven and slid the pan of yeast rolls in.

"Good gracious, that smells good." Laurie Emerson paused

as she entered the diner's kitchen and took a deep breath. "I don't see how you can bake as well as you do and not gain weight. If I could cook half as well as you do, I'd be a house!"

"Just because I can make it doesn't mean I can afford to eat it," Kate said with a grin, scooting the banana bread to a cooling rack.

Laurie pulled an apron off the linen shelf and tied it at her waist. "By the way, what happened to all those chocolate eclairs you were making yesterday morning? Did we sell out? I was hoping to snitch one for dessert last night."

"Oh, sorry," Kate said as she took down a mixing bowl to start the glaze for her cinnamon buns, a breakfast favorite for the diner's patrons. "I made those for a customer as a thank-you gift. He, uh…helped Janet and me out the other night."

Laurie cocked her head and raised her eyebrows. "He? You wouldn't be talking about that good-looking bodyguard that was in here yesterday with Senator Kelley, would you?"

Kate felt her cheeks heat with a blush, and a sappy grin tugged her mouth. "Well…"

"Uh-huh. I saw you talking to him. So…what's the story?"

"The story is we've got hungry ranchers to feed, ladies," Pete called from the grill behind them. "Gossip on your own time."

Laurie waved a dismissive hand at him. "Aw, pipe down, old man. I'll get to the customers in a second. It's not every day our Katie has a new beau!"

The heat in Kate's face prickled hotter, and she sputtered a laugh. "He's not my beau! I just wanted to thank him for his help."

"Who's not your beau?" Janet asked as she swished through the swinging door from the dining room.

"Hank Kelley's bodyguard," Laurie said at the same time as Kate said, "Never mind."

Janet frowned at her. "Did he ask you out?"

Kate rolled her eyes. "No!" Then to Laurie, "See what you started?"

Chuckling, Laurie headed toward the dining room. "You could ask him out, you know. It's the twenty-first century, Kate."

"Thanks for the tip," she called to Laurie's retreating back. "And in the twenty-first century, no one says *beau* anymore!"

Janet followed Kate to the refrigerator where Kate took out the butter and milk. "What did I miss? You're not really thinking of getting involved with that guy, are you?"

Kate shot her sister a give-me-a-break look.

"I mean, he's only in town for a while. And he's so... gloomy," Janet persisted. "He doesn't smile, and those eyes..."

Setting the milk and butter next to the mixing bowl, Kate pictured Gage's eyes. Dark blue. Piercing. So intense. Her pulse fluttered, remembering how his gaze had captivated her, had felt like a physical caress.

Her hand trembled as she measured out a half cup of milk for her glaze. "I don't know if anything will happen with him. I admit, he's rather serious. But I think he's handsome and polite. And don't forget how he stood up to Larry on your behalf."

Janet scoffed and leaned closer, pitching her voice low. "Yeah, and for his efforts, I got the third degree from Larry when we got home and a black eye. Lot of help he was."

"At least he got involved. That's more than most of the people in this town will do." Kate sliced off a large chunk of butter and put it in a small saucepan to melt.

"Because our marriage is our business and no one else's. I don't need every busybody in this town sticking their noses in my affairs."

Kate pulled the can of confectioners' sugar down from the shelf and pried off the lid. "Well, I'm glad he stood up to Larry. Larry needs to know he can't get away with treating you the way he does. It's criminal! I don't understand why you can't see what—"

Janet groaned and walked away. "Save your breath. I've heard that lecture before."

Kate's shoulders sagged in frustration. *You've heard it, but you haven't really listened.*

Giving the melting butter a brisk stir, she added a splash of vanilla and a heaping scoop of the powdered sugar, then slowly poured in the milk. She took out her restless energy on the concoction, whisking the ingredients until the mixture made a smooth glaze. With a satisfied sigh she set the pan of glaze aside and checked the cinnamon rolls in the oven. As always, baking soothed her, centered her. She missed the Zooks, her best friend Emma's family, and cooking made her feel closer to her Amish surrogate family and the ideals that they had taught her—ideals that gave her peace and strength and a moral grounding. All of which had been lacking in her own broken and loose-knit family.

The cinnamon buns were a golden brown, so she pulled them out and set them on the counter. As she drizzled the glaze over the hot buns, her thoughts drifted to Gage. Had he liked the eclairs she'd sent home with him? Would he stop by the diner again today?

She remembered his drastic reaction yesterday to what he'd clearly believed was a gunshot. Sure, his job was to protect the senator. To act first and differentiate noises later. But in the aftermath of his scramble to guard the senator from the perceived attack, Gage's mind had gone somewhere truly frightening. She'd seen the distant look, the terror, the panic in his face.

Absently, Kate swiped the dribble of icing from the pan as she returned it to the stove and licked her finger. What had spooked Gage? What threat hung over the senator so that he felt he needed twenty-four-hour protection? And had the senator, by coming to Maple Cove to escape the threat, instead brought a new danger to her little town?

Gage stuck close to Hank the next day, unable to shake the sense that the broken window at the bunkhouse last night had something to do with the people blackmailing the senator. Since Hank did little besides answer correspondence on his laptop from the desk in his guest suite and wander through the main house talking to his assistant, Cindy Jensen, on his cell phone, Gage fought a mammoth case of boredom by midafternoon. He knew he was lucky to have an assignment as cushy as guarding the senator, but he couldn't help but think of his fellow soldiers who were still in harm's way overseas.

Rather than dwell on the war that spawned his nightmares, Gage called to mind his brief encounters with Kate Rogers. After a long, dull day with Hank, perhaps he'd treat himself to dinner at Ira's Diner. He had no reason to believe she'd be working that evening, but if he could get out of the ranch house, away from Hank's droning about budgets and two-hundred-dollar-a-plate charity luncheons and funding for special projects, he'd be happy.

When Hank's phone rang for the umpteenth time that hour, Gage settled in on the family room couch and watched the man pace in front of the picture window that gave a panoramic view of the ranch property. He tuned Hank out and sank back into the sofa cushions. His mouth watered as he wondered what sort of desserts Kate had prepared for the diner today. Then his mind's eye pictured her graceful, feminine curves and bright smile, and a different sort of hunger fired inside him.

The frantic snapping of fingers jerked him out of his daydream, and he whipped his attention to the senator's frenzied hand gestures, pointing to the phone at his ear. Instantly, Gage recognized the stress in Hank's voice, saw the color leach from his face.

"No, don't do that!" Hank plunged his fingers into his hair. "I need more time." Raising his gaze to meet Gage's, the senator mouthed, *the kidnappers.*

Speaker, he mouthed back and leaned forward, perching on the edge of the couch.

Hank nodded and punched a button on the cell as he said, "I want to talk to Lana again. I need to know she's safe, or we have no deal."

"Keep it short," a male voice growled through the line, though whether to Hank or to Lana, Gage couldn't be sure.

Soon after that, a female voice carried through the static on the line. "Dad, it's me."

"Lana! Darling, have they hurt you? Where are you?" Hank asked, his voice cracking.

"I know you were always closer to the capital than you were to your children," Lana said, her voice remarkably cool and composed, "but when this is over, I hope we can spend some time together, maybe accept Mr. Bradshaw's offer to—" Lana gasped.

Hank's nose wrinkled. "What? Lana, are you—"

"Time's up," the male voice barked. "You know what to do if you want her to live."

With a click, the man was gone, and the buzz of a dial tone hummed through the line.

Hank wilted into the closest chair, his complexion pale. "If anything happens to my girl because of my stupid mistakes…" He let his voice trail away and pinched the bridge of his nose.

"Did anything she just said mean something significant to you? Who is Mr. Bradshaw?"

The senator said nothing for several seconds, and when he lifted his head, his eyes were suspiciously red.

Gage shifted on the couch, uncomfortable having the senator's emotions so near the surface.

"I assume she means Ernie Bradshaw, the owner of ELB Insurance. We saw him a few months ago at a dinner party at the state capitol. He invited us to use his cabin in northern California for a long weekend sometime."

Gage sat taller. "Where in northern California?"

Hank waved a dismissive hand. "Somewhere near the Nevada border. Around Lake Tahoe, I think." Hank sighed and shook his head. "I remember he said something about it being close to home in case something came up and I had to get back quickly."

"Home being Beverly Hills?" Gage clarified.

"Yeah. Beverly Hills is a lot closer to Nevada than D.C. is, now isn't it?" Hank said with an impatient sneer.

Gage ignored the man's snide retort and let Lana's comment replay in his head. *Closer to the capital than to his children.* Hank's children were far-flung now—running the ranch here in Maple Cove, studying abroad, serving in the military, working in Los Angeles. But by *capital,* did she mean D.C. or the state capital in Sacramento? The Bradshaws' cabin would be closer to Sacramento than any of his kids were.

"Working on the assumption that she's still trying to send us a message about where the kidnappers are holding her," Gage steepled his fingers and tapped them against his lips as he thought aloud, "I think we can rule out the mountains here around the ranch."

Hank furrowed his brow. "You think she was giving us another clue?"

"If I were Lana, I'd use my one shot at talking to someone as a means of sending a message that might help in my rescue. If she's as smart as you claim, I'd bet that's what she's doing."

Hank gripped the armrests of the chair he'd dropped onto. "So what does it mean?"

Gage twisted his mouth as he mulled the possibilities. "She wouldn't have mentioned Mr. Bradshaw if it weren't significant. Remember that as soon as she mentioned his name she gasped and was cut off."

"She said something her captors didn't like. Gave too much away."

Gage shrugged. "Maybe."

Jaw tightening, Hank surged to his feet to pace again.

"If they hurt her, so help me, I'll…" he thundered, clenching a fist to pound the air.

"When we take her last comment, which seemed to say she was in some remote mountains—" Gage stood and stroked his chin as he crossed to the senator "—and factor in this last comment, my gut says she is at this Ernie Bradshaw's cabin in the mountains. It's nearer to Sacramento than to where any of your kids live, it's remote, and it's at a high elevation. Am I right?"

Hank's face creased as he processed Gage's reasoning. "Sounds about right." The man's back stiffened, his eyes flaring with determination. "If we know where she is, then I can do something to save her."

Gage drilled a hard look on the senator. "You can call the FBI and let them handle this." Already Hank was shaking his head, frowning, but Gage persisted. "Tell them what you know, what Lana has said, and let the FBI—"

"No! I told you, I have my own resources. I've been in touch with a private contractor who can—"

A scoff ripped from Gage's throat. "A mercenary? You're going to send a mercenary in after your daughter? One guy against God knows how many men that are holding her?"

The senator matched Gage's steely stare. "He comes highly recommended. Ex-Special Forces. Discreet."

Gage sighed and shook his head. "With all due respect, sir—"

"Enough!" Hank Kelley aimed a finger at Gage's nose and narrowed his eyes to slits. "She's my daughter, and I'll handle this the way I see fit. Your job is to protect me, not to give me unsolicited advice."

Gage rolled his shoulders and firmed his jaw. But said nothing. He was a soldier, and he knew how to take orders. Even when he disagreed with those orders. "Yes, *sir.*"

Hank dug in his pocket and fished out a small notebook, which he flipped through until he found what he needed. He punched a number on his phone, held the cell to his ear.

Gage took a seat again, giving his head a small shake of disgust. The stubborn, foolhardy man...

"Garrison? Hank Kelley. I have reason to believe Lana is in the mountains near Tahoe. I want you to leave immediately. I'll send the exact GPS coordinates within the hour. Yes. I'll transfer the rest of the money to your account when I hear she's safe."

Gage sighed. Hank was sending his mercenary into the lion's den with a pork chop around his neck. He just prayed Lana wasn't killed in the crossfire.

Chapter 5

By Thursday afternoon, Gage had grown weary of listening to Hank grumble about the lack of response from his mercenary. He'd heard nothing in the thirty hours since he'd dispatched the man, and the senator's restlessness and grumpy disposition were wearing thin.

Or perhaps it was Gage's own repetitious thoughts, which vacillated between the horrific images and self-incriminations of his last mission in Afghanistan and the sweet flirtation and refreshing smile of a certain engaging pastry chef that wore on him. Gage was eager for the opportunity to visit Ira's Diner again. And not just because he recalled Kate saying she made chocolate layer cake on Thursdays.

As soon as his shift ended and he was sure Bart was set to guard the senator, Gage went in search of Ben, the ranch hand he'd talked to the night of the security breach. He found the hand in the stable, grooming one of the horses.

"I was wondering if I could borrow one of the ranch

vehicles to go into town," Gage said once the requisite pleas-
antries had been exchanged.

Ben jerked a nod. "Sure enough. Rusty said to make his
truck available to you or the other guard if you had need of it."
He gave the horse's flank a pat and put the grooming brush
on a shelf. "Follow me. The key is up at the bunkhouse."

Gage fell in step with Ben and remembered the damage to
the window the other night. "Have you heard anything back
from Sheriff Colton about the sabotage to the bunkhouse?"

"Only that his men couldn't find any fingerprints on the
brick, and the footprint seems to be from a pretty common
brand of athletic shoe. Size eleven." Ben removed his wide-
brimmed hat and wiped sweat from his forehead, despite the
cool October air. "I replaced the window this morning, once
the sheriff got all the pictures and evidence he wanted."

"What did Cole have to say about it all?"

Ben shrugged. "Just asked to be kept informed. I told him
there was no need for him to come back early from roundup.
Everything was under control here."

"And the roundup crew is due back when?" Gage asked.

"Sometime Sunday probably." Ben crossed the wood-plank
porch of the bunkhouse where a line of mismatched rocking
and Adirondack chairs waited for the return of tired ranch
hands. From the porch, the ranch hands had a breathtaking
view of the nearby mountains and the windswept valley where
the cattle grazed.

As Gage waited on the porch, admiring the view, a cool
October wind and the memory of rocky barren mountains
in Afghanistan sent a chill deep into his bones. An eagle
swooped low over the pasture and squawked loudly before
riding an updraft into the clear sky again. The sky was the
same bright, pale shade of Kate's eyes and...

Gage stopped in mid-thought and snorted a wry laugh
at himself, scuffing his shoe on the dusty porch. *Geez,* he

sounded like a lovesick teenager. Either he'd been without a woman longer than he wanted to admit, or he had it bad for Kate, if he was seeing her in every landscape and thinking of her throughout the day. Either way, he had to get his act together. He couldn't let a pretty face and some good food distract him from the job he'd been hired to do. The vandalism of the bunkhouse and threats made by Lana's kidnappers were enough proof that Gage had his work cut out for him.

He'd let his squad down on that isolated mountain road in Afghanistan, but he'd take a bullet to the head himself before he failed in his responsibilities again.

Ben returned, his footsteps making hollow thuds on the porch. "Here ya go. Rusty's got her parked behind the barn."

Gage took the key Ben extended to him and with a word of thanks, headed to the barn in search of Rusty's vehicle. The truck turned out to be a worn-out Ford truck circa 1970 or so. The front seat had been patched with duct tape and the body bore numerous spots of rust and faded paint. Dirty leather gloves and an odd assortment of chains and muddy tools littered the passenger-side floor. But when Gage turned the key, the engine roared to life. A working engine and four good tires were all Gage needed to get him into town...although he did park a block away from Ira's Diner. Kate didn't *have* to know about the battered vehicle he'd driven into town.

The bell above the door tinkled as he strode into the dining room and swept a gaze around the diner looking for one face in particular. Instead of Kate, he spotted Janet behind the counter, and his heart sank. For a moment he considered walking back out and getting his supper elsewhere, but Janet spotted him and waved him to the counter.

"I've got a seat for you right here, handsome." She patted a stool and gave the counter a quick swipe. "We missed you yesterday. What happened to you?"

Gage took a seat on the stool she offered and shrugged. "Had business to take care of at the Kelley ranch."

Janet leaned on the counter and gave him a seductive grin. "What sort of business? Anything juicy?"

"No." Gage gave her a quelling look. He had no interest in Janet to begin with and less interest in provoking the ire of her jealous husband. The woman's eye still bore evidence of the last time Larry had caught his wife flirting with him. "Kate here?"

Janet's grin faltered, and her jaw set. "She's in the back. But she's busy." Janet straightened and took her order pad from her apron pocket. "I'll take your order when you're ready. The special today is ham and navy beans with biscuits."

"Works for me. And coffee. Black."

The door to the kitchen swung open, and Kate breezed out carrying a chocolate cake. Her steps slowed when she spotted him at the counter and a bright smile bloomed on her face. "Gage!"

He nodded toward her, the hint of a grin tugging his lips. "And I'll take some of that for dessert." He left it to their imagination whether he meant Kate or the cake. At this point he'd take either. Both.

His frosting-licking fantasy roared through his mind and kick-started a hungry thrum in his blood.

Keeping her gaze on him, Kate slid the cake into the refrigerated dessert display case and sauntered over to greet him. Before Kate could so much as greet him properly, Janet's mouth firmed in a peckish frown, and she intercepted her sister, bodily blocking her.

"Gage is having the special. You need to get a fresh batch of biscuits in the oven."

"Just took some out a minute ago. Pete's got them." Kate leaned to glance past Janet and sent Gage another smile. "How are you tonight? Hungry, I hope. I'd hate to have to throw out any of my biscuits."

Janet placed a hand on her sister's arm and pushed her toward the kitchen. "I'll take care of the customers. You get back in the kitchen where you belong. Go bake something, Miss Pastry Queen."

Kate shrugged out of her sister's grasp. "I've finished baking for the day. You know that."

Gage watched the exchange between the sisters with interest. The disdain in Janet's tone when she referred to her sister's baking talent reeked of petty jealousy.

"Then clean something or help Pete or—"

"Forget it, Janet. I'm off the clock. I've been here since 5:00 a.m. and baking since 4:00 a.m. I want to say hi to Gage before I go home." Kate strode past Janet, and the older sister glared daggers at Kate's back.

But when Kate stopped across the counter from him, bringing the scent of yeast and chocolate with her, Gage forgot all about Janet's posturing. The smile Kate gave him, as if she were truly glad to see him, not just being polite, warmed him from the inside out. How was it this woman he'd only met days ago could chase away the chill that had resided in him for months? Kate made him forget, if only for a while, the loneliness and sense of isolation that had burrowed deep inside him long before that devastating day on the Afghan road.

"Hi, Kate." He felt the answering smile that pulled at his lips, a strange sensation, seeing as he'd had so little to smile about in recent months.

"Hi yourself. What brings you into town tonight?"

"I remembered you saying Thursday was chocolate cake day. Since Cole Kelley is out on roundup, I figured someone needed to eat his slice."

"And you volunteered for the job?" she said, chuckling. "How noble of you."

His smile grew, and he winked at her. "I live to serve."

She laughed harder, her eyes sparkling with mirth, and his heart squeezed.

"Oh my stars, you smiled! I knew you could do it." She gave his hand a congratulatory pat. "It really complements the rugged cut of your face and makes those baby blues shine."

Gage sputtered a tight laugh, making a mental note to try to smile more around Kate, if she liked what she saw. "Really? I've been that dour?"

She tipped her head. "Maybe not dour. More like—"

"Cold, stiff, grim, stony…" Janet said, purposely leaning into Kate, pushing her out of the way as she reached past her for a handful of drinking straws. "Take your pick. They all fit."

Kate gaped at her sister and sent Gage an apologetic look. "Janet!" she scolded in a hushed but harsh tone.

Gage schooled his face, scowling his irritation at Janet's interruption and her blatant rudeness to her sister.

"Well, he has been all of those things when he was in before." Janet cast a matter-of-fact glance to Gage. "You asked."

"I was talking to Kate."

With a haughty sniff, Janet walked away, but she'd done her damage. Kate's sunny smile was gone, replaced by an awkward embarrassment. Janet had achieved what she'd intended, but Gage would be damned if he'd let it work.

Forcing a grin back to his face, he took Kate's hand in his and squeezed. "I might be persuaded to smile again if you bring me that cake now instead of later. Life is short, and all that jazz…"

Her face brightened with gratitude for his attempt to reclaim the light mood between them. "You have a deal, if…"

She paused, and her cheek dimpled as she cocked her head. "Tell me about the places you've lived. I've never been anywhere but Small Town, Ohio, and Small Town, Montana. Did you ever live in Europe?" Her eyes lit with intrigue.

He nodded. "I was in Germany for a year."

He prayed she didn't ask about his last tour of duty. He didn't want to rehash anything about Afghanistan for her. Those memories were still too raw.

But if he could capture her attention for a few extra minutes, he'd gladly tell her about his childhood in the Smoky Mountains and south Texas. His short stint outside of Denver before he was recruited into the army. His basic training at Fort Jackson and anything else she wanted to know about his travels prior to his last deployment.

Wide-eyed, she leaned forward, against the counter, her full focus on him. "Can you speak German?"

He hitched his head toward the cake in the dessert display. "Cake first. Then Germany."

She served him a thick slice of cake and brought him the ham and beans that Pete slid onto the order window. Surrounded by good food and savoring Kate's attentive gaze, Gage regaled her with tales of his travels and answered her questions about the culture, the food, the scenery. When new customers came in, she greeted the arrivals with a friendly smile.

Janet swished past with a tray of dirty dishes. "Get the Johnstones' order, would you, Katie? I'm swamped back here with dirty dishes, and my back is hurting from that fall I took last night."

When Kate sighed and started to leave, Gage grabbed her hand to stop her. "I thought you were off the clock."

Kate shrugged and glanced at her feet. "I am, but…"

"This fall she took last night…did Larry help her off her feet?"

Kate's gaze darted back to his, and she shushed him. "Not so loud." Her cheeks flushed, and she nodded. "I'm sure he did. She swears she tripped on the rug, but she knows I know the truth, so I don't understand why she makes up these stories to cover for him…" She waved a dismissive hand. "Anyway, it will only take me a minute to get the Johnstones' order, then I'll be back."

"Kate."

She stopped and met his frown.

"Don't let her manipulate you."

Flashing him a forced grin, she said, "It's okay."

But Janet's treatment of her sister was not okay with Gage. Kate had moved across the country and worked in the same small dead-end diner with her sister just so she could help Janet, try to get her out of an abusive relationship. How much more of her life had Kate put on hold for her sister? And Janet didn't seem to appreciate Kate's sacrifices for her.

A bubble of protective anger on Kate's behalf filled his chest. How much of his observations and conclusions did he share with Kate? He had her best interests at heart, and yet… he'd only met her a few days ago, had spent precious little time with her. His opinion of what was happening between the sisters was based on a few encounters. Perhaps he should keep his thoughts on the matter to himself for now. He really didn't need to get involved in a family matter that had nothing to do with him. His job in Maple Cove was to protect Hank Kelley. Period.

He only cared about Kate's situation because…

He sighed as he watched her smile brightly to the Johnstones and sashay back behind the counter to post their order for Pete. His heart thumped harder as she returned to him, her sunny smile in place.

Damn. He had to face the truth. He'd begun to truly care for Kate.

The last thing he'd wanted was to get emotionally involved with a woman. He wouldn't be staying in Maple Cove after the threat to Senator Kelley had been resolved. He didn't need to form ties that would be broken so quickly.

And his dark and twisted history, full of post-trauma nightmares and memories of unspeakable acts of war, could only taint a life as pure and sweet as Kate's. Her fascination with his mundane stories of traveling with the Army showed just what a sheltered life she'd led. Her best friend growing up had been Amish, for God's sake.

"She's the only real family I have, Gage," Kate said, jarring him from his reverie.

He realized, to his dismay, that he'd been staring at Kate. What had she seen in his face that made her feel the need to defend her actions, her relationship with Janet?

He shook his head. "Sorry. I have no right to judge. I only hate to see you taken advantage of."

Kate laughed, a clear, bubbly sound that reminded him of a mountain brook. "Janet's not taking advantage of me."

But caution and concern dimmed the light in her eyes. Irritation gnawed his gut, knowing his meddling had put those clouds and worries in her head. He gave himself a swift mental kick in the shin.

See, your association with her is already tarnishing her shiny disposition, her optimism and joy for life.

"What happened to your parents?" The words tumbled from his mouth before he could stop them. Curiosity about this woman overrode the good sense not to pry, not to stir up painful memories for her, not to entwine himself any more with her life.

She tucked a wisp of her dark blond hair behind her ear and drew a deep breath, as if for courage. "Our dad died when we were pretty young. He was a heavy smoker, and it caught up with him. Then our mom took a second job to make ends meet for us. She was gone from home more than she was around. Janet was old enough by then to babysit me, so we pretty much raised ourselves from our pre-teen years on."

"Is your mom still alive?" he asked quietly.

Kate shook her head. "She died about five years ago. It took the cigarettes a little longer to catch up with her." Her brow knitted in a deep frown, and she glanced toward the kitchen where Janet had disappeared earlier. "Janet smokes sometimes. Not a lot but…it drives me crazy. I can't stand the thought of losing any more family because of smoking."

The temptation to tell her Janet was in much greater peril living with an abusive husband sat on the tip of his tongue, but he bit the urge back. That kind of gloomy reminder was not what he wanted for Kate tonight.

"You've told her how you feel?" he asked instead.

She shrugged. "Sure. But she swears she doesn't smoke that much. She could quit any time. She just smokes to relieve stress. Yada yada…" She waved a hand. "I try to pick my battles with her. I really start sounding like a nag when I complain about her bad habits, her husband, her driving."

"Her driving?"

Kate pulled a face and rolled her eyes. "The worst! She follows too close, never uses her turn signal, cuts people off…well, don't get me started!" She gave a short dismissive chuckle and put a smile back on her face. "Enough about me! What's your family like?"

Gage grunted and took a large bite of cake to stall. He didn't want to talk about himself, but since he'd grilled her about her life, he figured he owed her the basics. "Boring, average American family. Dad is an accountant, Mom's a substitute teacher now that the kids are grown and gone. My sister is a married stay-at-home mom. They're all still in Texas. No story there."

He stabbed another bite of cake and let the sweetness melt against his tongue. Pure indulgence. Kate really was an extraordinary cook.

"So you learned to bake from your Amish neighbor?" he asked, hoping to get her off the subject of his life.

"Mm-hmm. Emma's mother. They were my surrogate family, since my own home life was…well, nonexistent. They taught me a lot. Not just cooking."

He listened as she talked about the Zook family, how she'd helped them with the farm chores, attended church with them, shared meals with them, even wore a *kapp* and a simple dress and apron when she worshiped with them.

The more Gage listened to her expound on her close ties to the family, whose pacifist religion eschewed modern conveniences and adhered to a strict moral lifestyle, the more uncomfortable he grew. His training was in war—death and destruction. If he dared to explore a relationship with Kate, he'd surely destroy the very innocence and gentle sweetness that drew him to her.

"Sounds like you wanted to become Amish, join their clan."

She chuckled, and the light in her eyes danced merrily. "At times, yes. I love the simplicity of their lifestyle, but… I'm spoiled. I could never give up my cell phone, television, cars, microwaves…heck, all electricity!" Her smile dimmed. "I think I disappointed them in that way."

A sadness filled her voice that plucked at his heart. Quickly he shoved the tender emotion down. Empathy blinded a soldier to his duty.

Stay on target. Stay on task. No distractions…

Yet he heard himself say, "You miss the Zooks, don't you?"

She glanced up, startled, her lips parting. "Every day. But…" She sighed. "…my life is here now. My family is here."

Gage cast a side glance to the tables where Janet wiped

chairs and sent her sister scowling glances. "And family is important to you."

She nodded. "It's the most important thing. Next to God. The Zooks taught me that."

He wanted to tell her that sometimes family was a detriment. Sometimes family would drag you down, hold you back, ruin your chances for happiness if you let them. He thought about the crappy way Hank Kelley had treated his family for years. Ignoring them, cheating on them, taking them for granted.

Not to mention the way Janet disregarded her sister's sacrifices.

But when he saw the conviction that filled Kate's face, thought of the loving family that had given her this mantra, how could he argue the point?

His cell phone vibrated at his hip, and he pulled it out to check the caller I.D. *Bart*.

That didn't bode well.

"Sorry," he told Kate, "I need to take this."

She nodded agreeably, and he raised the phone to his ear. "Prescott."

"It's Bart. You'd better get back to the ranch."

The other bodyguard sounded out of breath, and Gage's senses went on full alert. In the background, Gage could hear the screech of alarms. He fished a couple of bills out of his pocket and slid them across the counter to Kate, mouthing, "Thanks. Gotta go."

"I'm taking Kelley down to wine cellar as we speak," Bart said. "There's been another security breach."

"What do we know?" Gage asked Bart, who met him at the top of the stairs to the panic room/wine cellar.

"Not much yet. I've talked to Cole. He's thinking he needs to come back to the ranch early in light of these two incidents.

I assured him his father was safe, and we were assisting the sheriff in investigating the breaches. But he said there was a crew headed back in the morning with the first part of the herd, and he's coming with them."

Gage rubbed his chin. "All right. I saw the sheriff's truck outside. He's searching the grounds, I guess?"

"Yeah. One of the hands, Ben something, thinks he saw someone on an ATV down in a lower pasture. Sheriff Colton's gone out there with Ben to have a look. He asked you to make sure the buildings were secure. I have—"

"Damn it, woman! I told you not to call me anymore!" Hank's raised voice drifted up from the cellar.

Bart and Gage exchanged frowning looks and headed down the stairs together to check on the senator.

Off to one side, Hannah sat on a folding chair with her orange cat on her lap and a disgruntled frown on her face. She said nothing to the men as they came down the steps but tapped her foot impatiently.

Hank was red-faced and visibly tense as he paced the small aisle of the wine cellar, his cell phone at his ear. "No! Not a chance. I told you that last time you called." He glanced up as his bodyguards reached the bottom step, then turned his back and stalked away. "The heat is on me from the press, thanks to you and the others, and there's no way I can—" The senator stopped abruptly, and his back stiffened. "Is that a threat? Because I will not— Gloria? Gloria!"

With a growl, Hank snapped his phone closed and jammed it in his pocket. "Stupid bitch," he mumbled under his breath.

"Sir?" Bart stepped toward the senator. "Was that Gloria Cosgrove again?"

Hank jerked a nod.

Gage fingered the keys in his pocket. "What sort of threat did she make?"

The senator didn't answer at first. He prowled the cellar

restlessly like a caged tiger. "Nothing specific. She wants back in my life, and when I refused to meet with her, she swore she could make my life miserable." Hank shook his head and rolled his shoulders wearily. "As if it weren't already."

From the far side of the room, Hannah gave a sniff of disdain.

Gage refused to feel sorry for the man. He'd had the world at his feet. Wealth, family, power, prestige…and he'd squandered it all with selfish choices and greed. To Hank Kelley, the glass was always half-empty.

Kate Rogers, by contrast, had little family, a minimum-wage job, and limited real-world experience. Yet she remained cheerful and optimistic, making the most of her small-town life and offering her customers happiness with her smiles, her baking, her sunny disposition.

Admiration lashed his heart in a rapid-fire beat he couldn't dodge. Every day, his respect for Kate grew. Like a splinter under his skin, a painful question prodded him: Could he learn to be happy with the simple pleasures in life the way Kate did? Could he ever shed the sackcloth and tragedy of his life and find fulfillment in small joys such as fresh baked bread and the friendly greeting of a neighbor?

The walkie-talkie in Bart's hand crackled to life, cutting into Gage's thoughts. "Sheriff Colton to Bart Holden, over."

"Holden here. Go ahead."

"We've found the ATV tracks and the spot where they cut the fence. Ben Radley is making the repair to the fence, and I'm heading back up to the house, while my men make a mold of the track. Is Prescott back yet? I want to be sure the buildings are secure before I head back to Honey Creek."

"He's right here," Bart said.

"Good. Tell him I'll meet him in front of the stable in five."

Gage nodded to Bart and was headed up the stairs when a thought occurred to him. He faced Bart and hitched his head, silently asking the other bodyguard to follow him back up to the main level.

"Yeah?" Bart asked as Gage closed the door to the stairs for privacy.

"The timing of Gloria Cosgrove's calls to the senator seems a little more than coincidental to me," he said, his voice pitched low. "Last time she called to harangue him was Monday night when the alarm was triggered by the vandalism at the bunkhouse. So while we're busy chasing down the source of this security breach, she calls begging for a meeting with the senator? It smells foul to me."

Bart lifted his chin and grunted. "Good point. Warrants watching."

"Ask the senator if Ms. Cosgrove said *where* she wanted to meet him. It'd be nice to know where she is, or where she thinks he is."

"Got it." Bart tapped his forehead with two fingers as he headed back downstairs.

Gage met Wes Colton at the stable, and they began a systematic check of the outbuildings and main house, the sheriff leading the search. The stables were quiet but for the soft nickering of the animals housed there. As they passed through the wide center aisle of the stalls, the black barn cat shot out from an empty stall and raced into the night. Though he'd been trained not to let such surprises rattle his composure while in the heat of battle, the sudden movement still sent a quick jolt of adrenaline pumping through Gage's veins.

"Critter's a little jumpy thanks to the racket from the alarm," Colton said, pausing to stare out into the inky blackness of the night where the cat had disappeared.

Gage sent the sheriff a scoffing laugh of agreement. "Apparently. I hope you're not superstitious. Black cat crossing our path and all…"

Sheriff Colton adjusted his hat and continued to the back

entrance of the stable headed towards the barn. "Let's hope a cat is the worst thing that crosses our path."

Flashlights on, Gage and the sheriff crossed the ranch yard to the large barn where, according to the brief tour Gage had been given earlier in the week, calves were birthed in the winter and horse feed was stored year-round. As they approached, Gage heard a rustle off to the right and caught Colton's arm. He aimed his light toward the side of the building. "Over here," he whispered.

Silently they crept toward the corner of the barn, and Wes peered around the corner. Gage drew his gun. Waited.

Wes tensed. Dropped to a knee. Reached for his service revolver. "Sheriff's department! Get on the ground!"

Immediately Gage positioned himself above the sheriff. He leaned around the corner just far enough to see the dark figure lurking in the shadows and aimed his flashlight and his weapon on the target. The figure reached for a shotgun.

"Drop your weapon!" Gage barked. "Hands in the air!"

When the suspect hesitated, Wes added, "Do it now! Hands out, get on the ground!"

Finally the slim figure raised his hands and flattened himself in the dirt. "Don't shoot! I—I work here."

Wes jerked his head, signaling Gage to move in and subdue the man while he kept his revolver trained on the suspect. Moving swiftly, Gage pinned the man on the ground with a knee between the suspect's shoulders.

"Who are you? What were you doing back here?" Wes asked as he approached, whipping out his handcuffs.

"M-my name's Kenny. Kenny Greene. I work for Cole."

"You're a ranch hand?" Gage asked.

Kenny nodded. "Y-yes, sir."

Wes shone the flashlight at Kenny's face, swept the beam down the length of his body. "Why aren't you with the rest of the crew on roundup?"

"I was, but… I came back tonight. I, uh…had a migraine, and… I'd left my medicine here."

The sheriff motioned for Gage to trade places with him and, once switched, he gave the young ranch hand a quick frisk.

"So why are you out here behind the barn?" the sheriff asked. "And why did you reach for your shotgun?"

"I—I was startled. I heard the alarm and came out to search the grounds."

The guy was clearly nervous, and now that they were closer, Gage could see that he was barely more than a kid. He couldn't have been older than twenty-two. Wes finished patting him down, then turned the young ranch hand over to Gage again. "I'm just gonna verify your story with Cole. Sit tight."

Gage kept his hand between Kenny's shoulder blades, his fingers twisted in the guy's shirt, while the sheriff talked to Cole. Only when Wes gave him a nod did he release the young ranch hand.

Over the next half hour, Gage and Wes finished searching the buildings but found nothing suspicious beyond the ATV sighting and the cut fence Ben had reported.

"Could just be kids, troublemakers who know the hands are away on roundup, but…" Wes sighed. "Considering the senator is here and this is the second callout this week, I'm not yet ready to write this off as simple juvenile mischief." He promised to be in touch with Cole for a thorough briefing when the rancher got back in town.

Gage considered filling the sheriff in on his theories regarding Gloria Cosgrove, but he decided he needed to do some more of his own research on the woman before he sounded that alarm. Stretching his tired muscles, Gage trudged back into the main house, said good-night to Hannah and Pumpkin, and headed down the long hall to his guest room. Before he went to bed, he wanted to see what the internet had to share about the mysterious and cloying Gloria Cosgrove.

Chapter 6

Friday morning Hank donned a pair of jeans and a casual shirt and announced he was going horseback riding. Which meant Gage was going horseback riding.

Though Gage had ridden a horse a couple of times in the past, low-key trail rides through national parks with his family while growing up hardly felt like proper preparation for riding out into the rugged Montana foothills with the senator.

"I thought all of the able-bodied horses were out with Cole on roundup," Gage said as he shadowed Hank's steps toward the stable.

"I board my stallion here year-round with specific instructions he's not to be used for ranching chores. He's a thoroughbred. Champion stock. Cost me a fortune, but I'd hoped to get stud fees for him."

"I take it that hasn't panned out?"

Hank grunted. "Not the way I'd hoped."

"Why not sell the horse then?"

"Because he's a magnificent animal. Wait until you see him." Hank led the way into the stable where they found Ben Radley saddling up the horse he'd been working with on Monday night.

"Morning, gentlemen," Ben said, tightening a stirrup. "What can I do for you?"

"I'd like Sultan and another horse saddled up. Gage and I are going for a ride."

Gage gritted his teeth at the highhanded manner in which Hank issued his order. Ben was not one of the senator's lackeys and had no responsibility to jump when Hank ordered.

"If it's not an inconvenience," Gage added, giving Ben an apologetic look.

"Well, I can get Sultan ready for the senator, but I don't have any other horses for Mr. Prescott. The ones that were left here during roundup were left because they can't be ridden for one reason or another."

"What about this one?" Hank pointed to the brown horse with the white nose that Ben had been saddling.

Ben shook his head. "Blaze is my horse, and I was just about to ride the fence and look for any other places where the vandals last night might have cut the wire."

"Can't that wait?" Hank asked, and Gage read the irritation on Ben's face.

"Not really. Cole's bringing four hundred head of the herd back today, and he needs a secure pasture to put them in."

The senator visibly bristled, clearly not used to being told no. Hiking up his chin, he peered down his nose at the ranch hand. "Then I'll ride the fence. That way Gage can ride your horse. Surely you have something else that needs to be done before Cole gets back?"

"Senator Kelley," Gage said quietly, "Perhaps another time would be—"

"What do you know about riding or repairing fence?" Ben cut in.

Hank chuckled. "Young man, I grew up on this ranch. My father taught me how to ride and rope and fix fences before I started school."

Gage regarded the senator with a lift of his brow. He'd forgotten that this ranch belonged to Cole's grandparents, meaning Hank had been raised here. Somehow the arrogant, self-centered senator didn't mesh in Gage's mind with the laid-back, rugged sort of man who worked a ranch. What had happened to change the senator? Did Hank ever miss the ranching life?

As it had last night, the comparison between Hank's high-maintenance, unhappy life and Kate Rogers's uncomplicated existence struck a nerve in Gage. Now that he was back in the States, starting a new life for himself, how did he avoid making the mistakes Hank had made that had led him down the path to such recklessness and dissatisfaction? Could Kate teach him a thing or two about finding purpose and contentment in a simplified world?

"All right. You've got a deal."

Ben's voice tugged Gage back to the conversation in the stable. He blinked and divided a look between the senator and the ranch hand.

Ben handed him Blaze's reins. "I took him out last night for a while. He seems to be well past his colic. But if he acts overly tired, bring him back in. Got it?"

How was he supposed to tell if the horse was "overly tired?"

"I know what I'm doing," Hank said, giving Ben a self-assured look.

Gage hoped Hank knew what he was doing, because Gage sure didn't.

As soon as Sultan was saddled, Hank and Gage rode out

onto the ranch property, and Gage marveled at the splendor of the sun spilling over the ridge of mountains. The peaks of the mountains in the range to their north already bore a cap of snow. They crossed a sprawling pasture where golden bales of hay in large rolls dotted the field, and a chill wind swept down from the hills, hinting of the winter that would arrive all too soon.

Gage inhaled deeply, his nose filling with the scent of leather, fresh air and fecund earth. For months he'd been surrounded by the exhaust fumes of military trucks, the smell of gun oil and deafening blasts of machine guns and explosives.

Patches of frost lingered on the grass in the pasture and sparkled like diamonds in the early morning sun. Nature seemed to be showing off this morning, pulling out all the stops to impress him.

Kate would love this view.

He twisted his mouth in thought and knitted his brow. Why was he viewing the world in terms of what Kate might think? He was in an open field where a sniper could be hiding, but he was considering how Kate might enjoy the morning vista at the Bar Lazy K Ranch. Sheesh.

Get your head in the game, Prescott.

"So what is our objective with this ride, sir?" he called to Hank, who rode well ahead of him. He needed to catch up to Hank, but he wasn't sure how to get his horse to move faster. He tried giving Blaze a little kick with his heel.

"Relaxation is my objective," Hank called back. "I need to think, get things straight in my head." He paused then added, "But since I agreed to check the fence, we're also looking for damage. When Cole brings the herd back, they'll be put in this pasture to graze."

Gage was uncomfortable with the distance that was

growing between his horse and the senator's. He could hardly protect Hank if he kept trotting off so far ahead.

"Go, horse! Giddyup!" Gage slapped the reins on Blaze's shoulder, and the horse picked up his pace for a few steps, then settled back into a lazy walk. "Senator Kelley, slow down. I need to stay with you, and this horse seems to only have two speeds, slow and slower."

Hank glanced behind him and chuckled. "Greenhorn."

Gage gritted his teeth and was considering issuing another warning to the senator when they reached the set of ATV tracks left in the dirt the night before. Ben's handiwork, repairing the damaged fence, was obvious as well. "Sir, the people who cut the fence here and went joy-riding on the pasture might have been testing the security system. The people responsible could be watching the ranch, monitoring your movements right now. We don't know that the people who cut the fence last night and broke the bunkhouse window weren't the same people who have threatened you."

Now Hank reined in his horse. "How would anyone know I was here? I've only told my closest associates and family that I'm staying with Cole."

"You've hardly kept a low profile while here. The first day you went into town for lunch. You're out in plain view of telephoto lenses and sniper scopes now. And cell phone calls are easily traced. You've had your phone glued to your ear since we arrived, despite our request that you not make calls." Gage tugged the brim of the ball cap he wore down to better shade his eyes. "Honestly, sir, you're not making my job easy when you defy our recommendations. You're incredibly exposed out here."

The senator sighed, and his shoulders sagged. Then with a deep inhalation, his chin came back up, and he stiffened his spine. "I won't be turned into a prisoner in that house. I won't give these people that kind of power over me!"

"You mean the way Lana is a prisoner?" He knew it was a low blow, but the man needed a wake-up call.

Hank turned angry eyes toward Gage. "You impertinent ass."

"Maybe so, but have you thought about how you are jeopardizing the safety of those around you? When are you going to shelve your pride and tell me what is really going on? Who is threatening you? Why are they threatening you? What do they want?"

Hank's face shuttered. "I can't talk about it."

"Meanwhile, your silence is putting Lana, Cole—hell your whole family—at risk. They went after Lana, so what's to stop them from gunning for any of your other children or your wife? Is that what you want?"

"Hell, no! Of course not! But this is a delicate matter with higher stakes than you could imagine. I have to handle this my way!" With a kick of his heels and flick of his reins, Hank took off with his stallion at a canter.

Gage slapped his reins and nudged Blaze's flanks with his heels, but the horse only moseyed along at a sedate pace, leaving Gage farther and farther behind Hank. He huffed his frustration with the senator, with his inexperience on a horse and with his sense that something terrible would happen to Hank if he didn't let Gage and Bart do their job properly.

Hank and Gage returned to the ranch a couple of hours later, having found no further damage to the fence of the lower pasture. As they rode up to the stable, Gage spotted Cole and a few hands unloading a trailer of cows and calves into a holding pen. Cole stopped what he was doing when he noticed his father riding up from the pasture and met them on their way to the stable.

"Welcome back, son. Looks like a productive calving season," the senator called to Cole as he reined his stallion and dismounted.

Cole stepped up to Blaze and caught the horse's bridle. "I suppose. What were you doing out there?" he asked, nodding toward the pasture.

Gage swung down from Blaze and muffled a moan of discomfort. Every muscle in his backside and thighs ached.

"I needed some air, and Sultan needed exercise." If Hank heard the suspicious tone of Cole's question, he didn't give any indication. "While we were out, we checked the fence in the lower pasture for Ben. It all looks good."

"You—?" Cole hesitated, then seemed to recall his father's upbringing, and gave a tight nod. "Thanks."

Hank patted Sultan's neck then headed back toward the house. "If you'd have one of your men put Sultan and the other horse up, I'm going to—"

"I don't think so," Cole interrupted, his voice loud and harsh.

Hank stopped, turned to his son, clearly startled.

Cole hitched his thumb toward the stallion. "Put your own horse up. My men are busy with ranch business, and they're on my payroll, not yours."

Hank frowned. "Then Ben—"

"Is helping me." Cole took Sultan's reins and held them out to his father. "I told you when you came here that I'd put you up for as long as you needed to stay, but I wouldn't let you interfere with the operation of my ranch. We're busy today, and will be for days to come as the herd's brought in from the mountains. You can tend to your own horse or you don't ride."

The senator lifted his chin, but his expression was contrite if awkward. "All right. I...can still put a horse up. Follow me Gage. I'll show you what to do."

Gage nodded to Cole as he took Blaze's reins and started into the stable, his gait slow and somewhat bowlegged.

"Prescott?" Cole called.

Gage paused, faced Cole. A grin dented Cole's cheek. "A soak in the hot tub will help those stiff muscles. Feel free to use the one up at the house."

Gage quirked a quick, wry grin. "I appreciate it. I'll do that tonight."

The following Monday night, hours after he'd retired for the evening, Gage answered a knock on the guest room door and found a rather unhappy-looking Hannah in the hall. She held out a phone to him and arched an eyebrow. "You have a phone call. In the future, I'd prefer not to be your answering service at this hour. Ask your lady friends to call your cell. You do have one, don't you?"

Gage blinked, caught off guard. Lady friends?

"Uh, yeah. I—sorry for the bother."

Hannah sniffed and turned on her heel.

Gage raised the phone to his ear. "Hello?"

"Gage? It's Kate Rogers, from down at Ira's Diner."

As if she had to explain who she was.

Gage's stomach flip-flopped, as if he were an adolescent with a crush, before he recognized the tremor in her voice that shoved giddy pleasure aside in favor of alarm.

"Hi. Is...something wrong?"

"I'm sorry to wake you at this hour. I called the ranch because I didn't know how else to reach you, but—"

"Kate, what's happened?"

She hesitated, sighed. "It's Larry. He hit Janet again."

Gage's hand tightened around the cordless phone. A white-hot fury coiled in his gut.

"They were fighting over something to do with money, and he snapped." Kate's voice trembled, and he longed to tuck her close and soothe away her fears. "She got away from him and came to my house, but I think he might come here looking for her."

"Damn," he muttered. Gage gritted his teeth, thinking of the two women alone at Kate's house and vulnerable to Janet's violent husband.

"I hate to ask this, but... I really don't know who else to call. No one else in town has been willing to get involved and—"

"What can I do?" he asked without hesitation. If Kate needed him, he'd move heaven and earth to help her. To protect her.

"It sounds silly, I know but—"

"Why don't you let me decide if it's silly. Talk to me, Kate."

"Can you come over? Stay with us? Just...just in case Larry shows up?"

"I'm on my way."

Twenty minutes after they'd hung up, the tall, dark and brooding bodyguard was on Kate's front stoop, filling her threshold with his broad shoulders and hard square jaw.

Kate clutched the edge of the door for support, because just the sight of Gage in his faded blue jeans and a gray Henley shirt made her weak in the knees. He sported a five o'clock shadow, and his mouth, as always, was pressed in a grim line. His hair looked damp, as if he'd recently showered, and guilt kicked her for having pulled him away from his evening routine. Had he been in bed already? Asleep, as she'd been when Janet had pounded on her front door?

"Thank you for coming," she managed to wheeze after taking a moment to find her breath. "Come in."

"No problem." He glanced past her as he stepped inside, bringing the crisp scent of autumn leaves and cool night air with him. "Any trouble since you called?"

"No. Janet was embarrassed to have you see her split lip, so she went to bed in my room."

Which left her alone with Senator Kelley's handsome bodyguard.

"You're sure this isn't an imposition? What about the senator? Aren't you supposed to be watching him?"

"Not until my shift starts at 6:00 a.m. I handle the day shift, and another guy covers the night hours."

She nodded awkwardly. "Oh."

Now what? She had little experience with men, much less with having one with so much magnetism alone with her. Emma's parents would probably frown on her entertaining a gentleman without a chaperone, but Janet was asleep just down the hall. That counted, right?

Gage walked into her living room, his gaze taking in her decor. She tried to see her home through his eyes, wondering what he'd think of her handmade quilt wall hanging, her basket of knitting by the couch, the simplicity and scarcity of decorations other than the ceramic pitcher and bowl set Emma had made for her their last Christmas together.

He wiped his hands on the seat of his jeans, drawing her attention to his backside. "Nice place."

Her pulse fluttered nervously. Had he seen her staring at his behind? "Uh, thanks."

She might have taken a vow of chastity until marriage along with Emma, but that didn't mean she was dead. She wasn't immune to a good-looking, testosterone-exuding male. "The house had been on the market for a couple years, and the previous owners were desperate to sell it, so I got it for a steal. It needed a little renovating but—" Oh, heavens. Don't let her start prattling like a ninny!

She bit her bottom lip to stop the logorrhea, and Gage's gaze dropped to her mouth, heat flaring in his navy eyes. Her heart answered by doing a little jitterbug, and, of course, she felt her cheeks flush.

She turned toward her kitchen, hoping to hide her school-girl reaction to him. "Can I, um…get you anything? A soda maybe?"

"No. I'm fine."

Wiping her palms on the legs of her flannel sleep pants—she hadn't wanted to look as though she'd dressed up for him, but now she worried that the pjs were a bit too informal—she led him into the living room and sat on the end of her couch. He sat next to her. Right next to her. Close enough that she could smell the remnants of soap from his recent shower. Close enough that she could feel his body heat enveloping her. He leaned back against the cushions and stretched his arm along the back of the sofa. The sleeve of his shirt tickled the nape of her neck, and Kate's toes curled. She was like a live wire, hypersensitive to his every move, his proximity, the whisper of his breathing in the quiet room.

As much as she'd hated calling him, imposing on him, she was twice as happy that he'd agreed. She'd waited for him with the tingle of anticipation a child would have on Christmas Eve. Had she used Janet's very real problem with Larry as an excuse to invite the intriguing newcomer in town to her home?

She chewed her lip again as misgivings bubbled up inside her. What did she know about entertaining a man? And what sort of compensation might he be expecting for his trouble?

"This happen often?" he asked.

Her gaze darted up to meet his. "Hmm?"

"Larry snapping. Janet coming over here in the middle of the night. Happen often?"

"Um, every now and then. More often lately. I think Janet tried to hide the truth from me at first, but now that I know, she comes over whenever she needs a place to retreat. Last time was about a month ago."

He nodded, his brow furrowed.

"And how often does Larry follow her over here? Put you in the line of fire?"

"About half the time."

"Do you call the police when he comes?"

"I have, but I think I mentioned before that Larry is chummy with most of the guys on our small force. He went to school with them, grew up with them. And Janet will never press charges."

A dark scowl puckered his brow. "I could handle Larry, given five minutes alone with him."

Kate bolted upright, her body tensing. "No! That's not what I asked you here for. Violence isn't the answer to violence. Beating on Larry only exacerbates the problem, feeds the cycle of evil."

He tilted his head, lifting his eyebrows and taking a long hard look at her. "The Zooks teach you that?"

She gave a tight nod. "The Amish are pacifists."

"And do you truly believe everything they told you, or are you just repeating what they believe because it sounds good?"

She folded her arms over her chest, affronted. "Are you suggesting I'm an empty-headed parrot, merely spouting back what I've heard without thinking things through for myself?"

His gaze flickered with some emotion—amusement? challenge?—and his eyebrows shot up. "I'm sorry. I didn't say that well. I meant no offense. I only wonder how closely your beliefs match what the Zooks taught you. How much you've accepted and integrated into your life, and what you've rejected as…" He seemed to fumble for the right word.

"Naive? Old-fashioned? Backward?" she offered. "The members of the Zooks' congregation have been called that and worse."

"And what do you call their lifestyle? Their beliefs?"

Kate relaxed again, leaning back into the cushions where Gage rested his arm. She considered moving but didn't want to appear…priggish. But the intimate seating arrangement made her more than a bit self-conscious, acutely aware of him in even the smallest ways. The crisp black hairs that peeked out at his collar, the masculine beauty of his hands and blunt-tipped fingers, the tiny lines that bracketed his mouth.

Not laugh lines. She didn't see Gage as the sort who laughed enough to have earned that distinction, a truth that speared a sadness to her core. Rather, she imagined the fine creases around his eyes and the firm line of his mouth were evidence of hard living. After all, he'd been a soldier. What kind of death and chaos had he witnessed while serving overseas?

She shivered, considering the differences in their experiences. She'd been sheltered, protected, immersed in the Zooks' simplistic lifestyle while Gage had faced the brutal realities of war and hardship. How could they possibly find any common ground?

Chapter 7

"Kate?"

Only when Gage spoke did she realize she'd been staring. At his face. His mouth.

And she'd never answered his question about the Zooks' beliefs.

She jerked her gaze to her hands in her lap and cleared her throat. "Well, I'd call the Amish lifestyle…refreshingly simple and unencumbered by the clutter of the modern world. And I think their beliefs—for the most part—are right on target. The kind of core family values that politicians espouse and too few truly live by."

Gage grunted and pulled a face, and she realized what she'd said. "Oh! I don't mean Senator Kelley. I mean, I wasn't saying—"

"Don't apologize on my account. The man cheated on his wife with multiple other women while portraying himself as a family man to his constituents. He's a liar and scum. My job is to protect him. Not agree with him or his choices."

She tipped him an awkward lopsided smile. "He has been a less than stellar role model at that. When Cole comes into the diner, he refuses to talk to anyone about his dad." Her shoulders sagged. "I don't think the senator was a very good father."

"And I think any comment from me on that point might constitute a breach of confidentiality."

He gave her a halfhearted smile, but even that hint of a grin was enough to capture her attention and set her pulse scrambling again.

"So…what aspect of the Zooks' beliefs *don't* you agree with?"

She tipped her head in thought. "Well, their views on the roles of women in society are rather…antiquated."

He hummed his agreement.

"And I don't think modern conveniences are sinful. On the contrary, in the middle of an August heat wave, air conditioning is a blessing. A gift from God, in my opinion." She angled a smile at him, and he nodded.

"No argument here."

"And I think their—"

Gage's fingers brushed the back of her neck, and she nearly came out of her skin. The rest of her thought vanished, the words disappearing from her tongue like sugar dissolved in hot water.

When he settled his hand against her neck and gently kneaded the muscles at her nape, a rush of sweet, hot sensation skittered the length of her body. Her scalp tingled. Her heart thundered. All her nerve endings jangled and fired.

Kate drew a steadying breath into her lungs. *Calm down. Don't make a fool of yourself!*

Easier said than done when his electric touch made her

want to roll over at his feet and beg for more like an eager puppy.

But good heavens, if she had a tail, it would be wagging. She swallowed hard, fighting back a moan of pleasure.

"Want to watch a m-movie?" she croaked, spoiling any illusion of composure.

"Sure. If you don't think the noise will wake Janet."

"It shouldn't. She sleeps pretty soundly. And we'll keep the volume low."

His courtesy, thinking of Janet's needs, touched Kate. The more she knew about Gage, the more he reminded her of a knight of old. Gallantry, courage, sacrifice…and a fine physique to go with it all. But why couldn't he bring himself to smile more often, to laugh, to enjoy life? What troubling event in his past had he been remembering the other day when the truck backfired outside the diner?

She wanted to ask him about it, but feared the question was far too personal for this stage of their relationship.

Relationship? she thought as she scooted off the couch and crawled a few feet to her video cabinet. The term made it sound like she was dating Gage, when in truth, he was merely doing her a favor, standing guard against Larry showing up and causing problems.

Yet, you've dealt with Larry on your own in the past, her conscience argued. *Why did you really call Gage tonight?*

She stared at the titles of her movies and frowned. If she were honest with herself, Larry had been an excuse to some degree. Sure, he could be violent and unpredictable. And sure, he scared her, worrying her as to how far he might go some nights when he was in a rage. And yes, Gage did make her feel safer, provide the extra security she craved for *just in case.* But she wanted Gage there, with her, for other reasons. She—

Gage's chest bumped her back, and she caught her breath.

He'd materialized behind her while she was distracted by her justifications. Now, leaning forward, reaching past her to pull a DVD from her collection, he said, "You have a lot of old movies here. Don't you like anything Hollywood is doing these days?"

"Well, nothing I think you'd like. I keep more recent movies in another cabinet, but they're mostly chick flicks."

"And what is it you think I'd like?" His tone was curiously light, and she turned to meet his gaze before answering. He arched one eyebrow, and a tiny grin tugged the corner of his mouth.

"I've got you pegged as a fan of guy-type movies, the kind with explosions and big guns shooting, and skimpily clad women who need the action hero to save them from their own stupidity."

"I have no objections to skimpily clad women. Rather enjoy them, in fact."

"I see." Kate turned back to the selection of DVDs again, feeling a blush rise in her cheeks thanks to the deep purr in his voice. Okay, she'd set herself up for that one....

"But I've actually had about all the explosions and gunfire I can take for the foreseeable future," he added quietly.

"Then what do you like?"

He grunted. "You promise not to laugh?"

"No." She glance back at him over her shoulder, a mischievous grin twisting her mouth. "I love to laugh. Especially if something is funny." She turned her body so she faced him more fully. "Is there something funny about the kind of movies you like?"

"Uh, well...something stupid maybe. Mindless and goofy." He took a deep breath as if bracing for a deeply personal confession. "I generally like the big, dumb comedies with the pratfalls and bathroom humor and blatant sexual innuendo and sight gags and main characters getting hit in the crotch or bit on the ass by a little Chihuahua or something. Frat party kind of humor."

She goggled at him. "Seriously?"

He lifted a corner of his mouth in an embarrassed-looking grin. "Afraid so. I'm not proud of it, but…well, those are the kind of movies that provide escape for me. If I watch a movie, I don't want heavy emotion or reminders of what's wrong with the world. I've lived the whole shoot-'em-up thing, so when I'm not critiquing the director for what he got wrong about warfare and guns, I'm thinking how I get enough blood and fighting in my real life."

Kate held his gaze, staring deeply into the fathomless blue depths and realizing he'd just bared a part of his soul to her.

After a moment, he seemed to realize this as well, and he jerked his gaze away, clearing his throat awkwardly. "Anyway, I doubt you have anything like that, so…we can watch whatever you want."

Kate drew an unsteady breath and considered the movies in her cabinet again. "How about *The Pink Panther?* The original movie with Peter Sellers?"

His face brightened, and he cocked one eyebrow. "'I thought you said your *dag* didn't bite!'" he said with a comical accent.

"'That's not my *dag,*'" she said, her lips twitching and her voice equally thick with accent.

His cheek twitched, then a chuckle rumbled from his chest. "Classic."

She added her chuckle to his, then thought of another silly scene from the movie and laughed harder.

"What?" Humor and curiosity lit his eyes.

She tried to tell him which of Peter Sellers's goofy antics had tickled her, but an uncontrolled fit of giggles overcame her, and all she could do was laugh and wipe happy tears from her eyes. Before long, he'd caught her case of giggles, and he loosed a rich melodic laugh to join hers. The sweet sound filled her, thrilled her, and the smile that sculpted dimples in his cheeks and laugh lines at his eyes transformed his face. When he smiled, Gage Prescott was simply breathtaking.

Without thinking, Kate reached for him and stroked a hand along the side of his face. "Oh, wow," she said breathless from her bout of giggles, "you should do that more often. You have a terrific smile."

Her palm slid over the scratchy stubble on his cheek, and the sensation sent a thrum through her. He must have sensed when she realized the intimacy of her touch, because right when she would have snatched her hand back, he covered her hand with his own and curled his fingers around hers.

"I'll have a smile for you anytime you ask," he murmured and carried her hand to his mouth. When he pressed a tender kiss to her palm, her body felt as if it had burst into flame, starting with a stinging blush in her cheeks. Her breath stumbled as it left her lungs, and she couldn't have pulled her gaze from his if she'd wanted to.

What was happening to her? She'd never been so forward with a man before, never been so enchanted by a pair of stormy blue eyes and the hard slash of a mouth. But suddenly all she could think of was how it would feel to have Gage kiss her. To kiss him back. And more.

On the street outside, a car door slammed, and the sound yanked her from her wayward thoughts. She tore her gaze from his and, with a shaking hand, slid *The Pink Panther* from her DVD collection.

"So…shall we watch it? I like to hear you laugh. You've been far too serious since you arrived in Maple Cove, Mr. Prescott. Life is too short to waste time frowning."

"Have I been that bad?" His hand rested on her shoulder then skimmed lightly down her arm as she moved away to her DVD player.

"Afraid so. There's a reason you've been so stingy with your handsome smile? Is guarding the senator really that nasty a job?"

She cued up the DVD and turned the television to the right channel.

"When I'm working, I need to be alert to everything around me, any possible hazard, and be prepared to act. I can't allow myself to be distracted by things that—"

"Make you smile?" she finished for him. "Is smiling, laughing, really such a drain on your attention?"

"Maybe it's not the smiling so much as *who* makes me smile and *why* that is distracting." He arched his eyebrow again and gave a little nod toward her.

She pointed to herself and mouthed, "Who, me?"

His face brightened, and she had her answer.

She made him smile? The idea sent a giddy trill through her.

The movie started, and she lowered the volume so they wouldn't wake Janet, then joined him on her couch. He draped his arm around her shoulders, and she leaned into his protective warmth, tucking her feet beneath her.

"Are you sure you want to watch a movie? Don't you have to get up early for the diner?"

"Normally, I do, but tomorrow is my day off—sort of." She sighed. "I have to do some baking for the diner in a couple of hours, but then I can nap. I can send the desserts and so forth to the diner with Janet."

She watched the movie, snuggled in the crook of Gage's arm and savoring the sound of his quiet laugh when the bumbling Inspector Clouseau caused one mishap after another.

When the movie ended, she rose reluctantly from the security of his arm around her and stretched to work the kinks from her muscles. "I have pies to bake and rolls to start rising. Want to help me?"

Gage flipped his wrist to check the time.

Kate's gut clenched guiltily. She'd monopolized his time for hours. "I don't want to keep you if you need to get back to the Kelleys' ranch. I just thought—"

He held up a hand to forestall her argument. "I'd like to see you in action. Lead the way."

Savoring the thought of a little more time with him, she took his hand and walked him to her kitchen where her baking pans and ingredients were already lined up waiting for her morning baking.

When they entered the kitchen, her cat, Sinatra, a pure-bred white Persian, stood in his cat bed and stretched. Sinatra meowed, requesting his breakfast, and before she started mixing up a batch of rolls, she poured her kitty companion a large bowl of food and set it on the floor.

Gage regarded the fluffy feline with an odd expression, and she wondered what he must think of her rather girly pet. The guys she knew generally avoided fluff-ball cats.

"What's wrong?" she asked when he continued to stare at the cat with a quirk in his brow.

"His eyes are different colors," he said, finally shifting his gaze from Sinatra to her.

"Yeah. I think it gives him character, but the breeder who owned him abandoned him because of his mismatched eyes. Then his second owner shut him out on a balcony overnight, and he fell three floors and was lost for two weeks before he showed up again."

Gage cocked his head and blinked slowly. "He fell three stories and survived?"

Kate nodded. "Survived, but is brain-damaged. He likes to stare off into space at nothing. Poor dumb guy." She ruffled Sinatra's long fur. "That he survived alone for two weeks with all the predator animals in these parts is pretty amazing, too. When his second owner decided to get rid of him, I adopted him. I felt sorry for the brain-damaged, mismatched-eyed goofball. Isn't that right, Sinatra boy?"

When she glanced up from patting her cat, Gage was staring at her, grinning. She tipped her head. "Now what?"

"You. Adopting an outcast cat, leaving your life in Ohio to protect your sister, feeding ranchers, baking eclairs for the new guy in town... You take care of everyone." He paused and his expression sobered. "But who takes care of you?"

His question burrowed to her marrow. In Ohio, she could say unequivocally that the Zooks had her back and took care of her when she needed someone. Since moving to Montana last year, she'd made friends, but none as dear as Emma and her Amish family. Her life, except for Sinatra, was rather lonely. She worked, then came home to sleep, then rose early to work again, holding down two jobs, as the diner's baker as well as a full-time waitress.

Without answering, Kate began arranging her bowls and measuring cups in preparation for making yeast rolls.

Gage moved up beside her. "Well, Kate? Does anyone take care of you?"

"I do."

"And?"

She shot him a glance. "Why? Are you volunteering for the job?"

Oh, heavens! Where had that come from? She didn't want him to think she was pressuring him for some kind of commitment!

"For as long as I'm in town, if I'm not on duty guarding the senator, I'm happy to help you out however I can."

Kate opened the storage jar of flour and dug several scoops out to dump in her bowl. All the qualifiers in his response spoke for themselves. His presence in her life was temporary. His priority was his job, and he was simply on loan to her during his off hours.

Though she knew all of this going in, the reminder stung. She'd let herself fall a little in love with Gage and all his charming, protective and honorable attributes. But she needed a man who would put family first. Someone who would stick around, not drift through town while on assignment. She needed someone who could give her his heart, who could open himself to her and share his deepest fears, aspirations and desires with her.

Which ruled Gage out on every count.

"That's the way. Great!" Kate said as Gage took over kneading the dough for the rolls with sharp thrusts of his palms. "You're a quick study, Mr. Prescott."

"It's not exactly rocket science," he said with a grin.

She lifted her chin with a haughty sniff. "Perhaps not, but I think good baking is an art."

As she turned back to the bowl of batter she was stirring, Gage swore he saw a frown line dimple her forehead. Had his comment hurt her feelings? The last thing he wanted to do was insult her profession, especially when she was so good at her job.

"Well, maybe I think it's easy because you're a good teacher." He cast a side glance toward her and bumped her hip with his.

"Thanks." The shy smile that curved her lips said he was forgiven.

As he worked the raw rolls, the dough started clinging to his fingers. "Is it supposed to be sticky like this?"

She glanced over. "Oh. No. It needs more flour." She dusted the counter and his hands with flour, stepped behind him and reached around, encircling him with her arms. Covering his hands with hers, she drove his palms into the dough. "Try it like this. Push the dough with the heel of your hand. Don't squeeze it."

For more than two hours, he'd helped Kate prepare baked goods for the diner—carrot cake, blueberry muffins, banana bread and cherry pie. Her kitchen smelled as though a bread truck had crashed into a fruit stand. All the sweet, fruity, yeasty scents that always clung to Kate now filled her home and made his mouth water. But the press of her petite body against his ignited more than his hunger. He longed to pull her close and kiss her flour-smudged face, sample her sweet strawberry lips.

Flipping his hands over, he laced his goo-coated fingers with hers, transferring the sticky mess to her hands. He let a low rumbling chuckle roll from his throat. "Gotcha."

"Hey!" she said laughing. "What are you doing?"

"Keeping you close. Right where I want you." He managed to pivot to face her without dropping her messy hands, then tugged her against his chest. She raised a wide-eyed look to him, blinking her surprise. The vein in her neck fluttered, giving away the quickening of her pulse. She nervously wet her lips, and his gaze locked on her mouth.

Damn but he wanted her! He dipped his head, heard her inhale a shallow, quick breath, and he brushed his lips along hers. A sensation like warm honey spread through his blood. His body hummed with building desire, and he felt her tremble.

"Kate..." he whispered, "I want—"

With a nerve-rattling trill, her phone rang and she pulled away. Her cheeks flushed bright pink, and her chest heaved as she gulped air. Stiffly, she moved to the phone on the counter. When she glanced at the caller ID, she frowned. Using the tip of one dough-covered finger, she punched the speaker button and said, "Larry, do you know what time it is?"

"Past time for Janet to get herself back home, that's for sure."

"She's asleep, like most people are at this hour."

"You're up."

"I'm baking for the diner. I always start early. I have to if it's going to be fresh each day."

"Whose truck is that that's been outside your house all night?" Larry asked.

Kate stiffened. "How would you know what's been parked at my house?"

"I drove by looking for Janet's car, of course."

"More than once, I take it."

"What if I did? Who you got in there with you?"

She glanced at Gage, then away. "I asked a friend to come over—not that it's any of your business."

"If Janet's there, it's my business." Larry mumbled something else under his breath then asked, "Is it a man? You got a man there? Is Janet sleeping with this guy at your house, thinking she can hide it from me?"

Kate rolled her eyes. "Janet is not sleeping with anyone at my house or anywhere else. Jeepers, Larry! When are you going to give her some credit and stop questioning every little thing she does? Your jealousy is wrecking your marriage… among other things." She added the last under her breath.

"It is a guy, isn't it? She's got a man in there, don't she?" Larry ranted. "Who is it?"

"Have you ever considered that if there *is* a man at my house, maybe he's here to see *me?*" Kate jammed her hands back into the dough and gave the mixture a vicious squeeze.

Larry laughed. "Saint Kate with a man? Miss Goody Two Shoes? Yeah, right. Hell hadn't frozen over last time I checked."

Gage had planned to keep his mouth shut and let Kate handle her brother-in-law on her own terms, but the hurt look that crossed her face gouged a deep swath through his soul. On sympathy's heels, protective fury ripped through him.

"Check hell again, pal," he said loud enough for Larry to

hear. "Satan's pulling out his winter gear. I'm a man. I'm here with Kate, and I have been all night."

Kate gasped and snapped her gaze to his.

"Who is that? Kate, what's going on?" Larry yelled through the line.

"Gage Prescott, retired U.S. Army Ranger, currently working security detail for a prominent client." Gage stepped closer to the phone to be sure Larry heard him. Anger pulsed through him like a poison. "I'm here because Kate asked me. And if I find out you've hit Janet again, I don't care how many friends you have on the police force, you'll have to answer to me. Got that, pal?"

Kate bit her lip and shook her head vigorously. "Gage, no!" she whispered. "Don't antagonize him!"

"What the hell business is it of yours what I do or don't do with Janet?" Larry raged. "I answer to no one but myself. She's my wife, damn it! You stay out of our business, or I'll make you wish you had!"

Before Gage could reply to the threat, Kate stepped close to him and pressed her gooey hand over his mouth. She shook her head, and her eyes pleaded with him not to engage Larry. The vulnerability and desperation in her gaze shot through him, leaving a sharp ache in his chest. No matter how her Neanderthal brother-in-law pushed his buttons, Gage could never do anything he thought would hurt Kate. He battled down his ire and frustration and gave her a nod of acquiescence.

"I'll tell Janet you called when she wakes up in a little while," Kate said, turning back to the phone. Immediately Gage missed the subtle press of her body against his. "I have to finish the baking for the diner now. Goodbye, Larry." She lifted the receiver and dropped it back in the cradle to disconnect the call, then faced Gage. "I'm sorry about that."

"You have no reason to apologize. I'm the one who lost my

temper with the maggot." He clenched his teeth and expelled a deep sigh. "He honestly thinks he has a right to knock Janet around because they're married? What kind of twisted, prehistoric thinking is that?"

She stepped over to the sink and rubbed her hands together. Bits of dough clumped and peeled off her fingers. "All too common, I'm afraid." Dejection weighted Kate's voice. "I've researched domestic abuse a good bit since moving here, trying to decide what I should do for Janet. I've located several good women's shelters in the area, but she has to *want* to go, to be committed to getting him out of her life. If she keeps forgiving him and going back to him, my hands are tied."

Gage joined her at the sink and copied her hand-rubbing technique to loosen the sticky dough. "I wish I could help."

She angled a melancholy smile at him. "I wish you could, too. Sometimes I feel really alone in all this. I don't even have Janet on my side. She fights me about leaving him, denies she has a problem, then drags me into the middle when it serves her purposes."

Alarm shot through him. "Puts you in the middle how?"

Visions of Kate being in harm's way from the violent brother-in-law churned his stomach.

Kate finished washing her hands and shook excess water from her fingers before grabbing the closest towel. "Like tonight, when she came here to sleep after their fight. Then he calls looking for her and I…" She shook her head again. "I'm sorry. I'm no better, dragging you into our personal problems. I shouldn't have asked you to come over, shouldn't be burdening you with all this."

He quickly dried his hands on the other end of the towel she used, then cupped her face between his palms. "I'm glad you called. I want to help. I want to be sure you're safe. Please,

Kate, if you ever think you're in danger from Larry, call me. Any time, day or night. I'll come."

Moisture puddled in her eyes, even as her cheek twitched with a sad grin. "Thank you, Gage."

She rose on her toes, brushed a quick kiss across his lips, then dropped her heels to the floor again and lowered her gaze. All the oxygen in Gage's lungs stilled, like the quiet before a storm. When she took a step back to move away, he caught her arm.

Her kiss had lit a fire in him, and shockwaves still rippled to his marrow. With a finger under her chin, he lifted her face and saw the tear that had broken free of her thick eyelashes. The sight of that tear sucker-punched him, and he hauled her closer, sank his fingers into her hair. Cradling her nape with a splayed hand, he dipped his head and whisked the tear from her cheek with his kiss. He absorbed the shudder that shook her, tasted the breathy sigh that whispered from her lips. Bowing his head, he covered her mouth with his...and was lost.

Chapter 8

When Gage pulled her against his wide chest, anchoring her head with his hand while he kissed the breath from her, all worries of Larry and Janet vanished. All strength left her legs. All thoughts of the diner's baking flittered away....

With the searing touch of his lips to hers, Kate became a pliant, single-minded sponge greedily soaking up the heady pleasure of being kissed by a man like Gage. Under the sweet assault of his talented mouth and persuasive tongue, she very nearly forgot every lesson about the value of chastity the Zooks had taught her. After one taste of Gage's kiss and the incredible sensation of his hands massaging her scalp, her neck, her shoulders, she was ready to abandon her vow of celibacy for even a few minutes of the nirvana Gage offered.

She clung to the rock-like muscles of his shoulders, secure in his embrace as he explored her mouth, her arched throat, the sensitive spot beneath her ear. His lips were tender while the day's growth of beard on his chin and cheeks scraped her skin. The dichotomy reminded her of Gage himself, so gruff and serious on the outside, but so clearly honorable and kind underneath.

His hand slid down her spine, settling his palm at the small of her back and pulling her closer. With her body flush with his, she could feel the thudding, steady beat of his heart, the warmth of his body heat, and—she gasped softly when realization dawned—the proof of his arousal nudging her belly.

He broke their kiss and gazed at her from under hooded eyes, his lips swollen and damp, much as she was certain hers were. "You okay?"

Breathless as she was, she couldn't find her voice, but she hummed a positive response and nodded. Heat prickled her cheeks. Would her naïveté and inexperience turn him off?

He traced the line of her chin with his thumb, and tingles raced over her skin from head to toe. She couldn't stop the tiny moan of pleasure that rattled from her throat.

He lifted one corner of his mouth in a lopsided grin. "My sentiments exactly."

As dreamily lethargic as she was, wrapped in his arms, his hands tantalizing her with tender caresses, she gazed up at him and reveled in the warmth of his smile. If only she could convince him to allow her past his iron defenses more often. If only she could win his trust enough to learn what sadness haunted him, robbing his life of joy.

The timer on her countertop dinged, reminding her of the pies that were baking, and disappointment pierced her like a deflating balloon. She wasn't ready to leave his arms, interrupt this moment, quit learning the texture of his kiss...

So instead of pulling away, she stretched up on her toes again and captured his mouth with hers. He greeted her with an equal enthusiasm, and his tongue teased the seam of her lips until she opened to his exploration. She followed his lead, discovering new and wonderful sensations with every touch, every squeeze, every nuzzle.

"Well, well. Isn't this cozy?"

Kate gasped and shoved away from Gage when Janet's voice shattered the silence. She jerked a guilty glance toward her sister, who stared at them from the door to the hall.

"I think I smell something burning." Janet nodded toward the oven, then gave them a saucy grin. "Or maybe that's just the smoke from the heat you two are making."

Gage released Kate and finger-combed his hair as he stepped back. "Janet," he said by way of greeting. The smile that had lit his eyes moments earlier was gone from his face, replaced with his stiff politeness.

Janet sauntered over to the idle coffeemaker and frowned. "No coffee yet?"

Flustered, Kate hastily straightened her shirt and hurried over to the coffeemaker. "Sorry, I got busy…sidetracked and—"

"Yeah, I saw your sidetrack." Janet arched one eyebrow, her expression at the same time peevish and teasing. She batted Kate out of her way. "Go on. Get your pies. I'll make the coffee."

Kate moved to the oven and pulled out the two slightly overbaked apple pies and slid them onto cooling racks. They weren't a loss, but when she thought of how easily she'd been distracted from her baking, she felt heat rise in her cheeks. She turned to Gage and pressed her hands to her flushed face. "I, um…need to finish a few things here before Janet leaves for the diner."

He nodded, his expression resigned. "I'll get out of your way."

As he started for the door, a flutter of uneasiness stirred inside her, a reluctance to see him leave, a sadness for the lost bliss of his embrace, an embarrassment for Janet's abrupt manner. "Gage, wait. I—"

When he paused, she wasn't sure what to say, but she spied the muffins cooling on her table and quickly wrapped two in a napkin. "Take these. Breakfast."

He allowed his hand to linger on hers as he accepted her offering, and his eyes held her gaze for an extra second or two before he turned to go. In that brief look, she swore she felt a connection to him, an understanding that something had changed between them, that their kiss was only the beginning of something bigger, deeper...scarier.

Swallowing the quiver of anticipation that seized her, she followed him to the front door. "Thank you for coming. I know I got you out of bed, kept you awake when you probably needed to be sleeping, imposed on your good gr—"

He laid a warm finger on her lips to hush her.

"You're welcome." With a quick kiss to her forehead, he breezed out into the brisk October morning and crossed her yard in a few long strides. She watched from her front stoop until the rattletrap truck he'd driven over turned a corner and disappeared from view.

"So you're rethinking that career as a nun I take it?"

She brushed past Janet, who chuckled and nibbled a muffin as Kate returned to the kitchen. "Bite me."

Janet barked a laugh. "I thought the bodyguard already did that."

"Don't you think you were rather rude to him just now? He came over here as a favor to us." Kate busied herself cleaning dirty bowls and pans.

"A favor? Looked to me like you were doing him the favor." Janet pulled the pot out from the coffeemaker before it had finished brewing and coffee dripped onto the burner and sizzled as she poured herself a cup.

"I asked him to come over last night in case Larry came by."

"And what? We'd have an orgy?"

Kate gritted her teeth. "In case Larry caused trouble. I didn't know how bad your fight was and if he might come looking for you and be a problem."

Janet scowled and touched her bruised jaw. "I don't want you blabbing my business to other people. Larry's not dangerous, he just has a bad temper."

Kate gaped at her sister. "*Just* a bad temper? Do you hear yourself?"

Janet folder her arms over her chest, her expression closed. "I only came here to give him time to calm down. He's not going to come over and give you trouble."

"He has before. And he drove by here last night at least a couple times. I know that much, because he called here a little while ago and asked about Gage's truck being out front."

Janet stiffened, alarm in her eyes. "What did he say?"

Kate frowned. "His usual suspicious crap. He thought you were seeing another man over here." Janet's eyes widened, and Kate quickly added, "Don't worry. I set him straight."

"Great." Janet's shoulders sagged as she unfolded her arms and picked up her coffee. "You have an all-nighter with your new boyfriend, and I catch the flak."

Kate bristled at the implication she'd done something unseemly. "I didn't—"

Janet snorted. "I'm surprised you even know what to do with a man. I thought you'd sworn to be celibate until you married."

"Gage isn't— We didn't—" Kate sputtered, hardly knowing where to start responding to Janet. "What's wrong with waiting for the man I want to marry?"

"I never said there was anything wrong with it. But unlike Emma, you're not Amish. You don't have to wait." Janet dug a cigarette and lighter out of her bathrobe pocket and lit up.

"I want to wait. I want it to be special. I—" Kate stepped

forward and tugged the cigarette from her sister's mouth. After stubbing it out in the sink, she sent Janet a stern look. "I've asked you not to smoke in my house."

Janet rolled her eyes. "Does the bodyguard know you're a no-go? He looked pretty eager when I walked in a little while ago."

Kate tossed a hand towel on the counter with an unsatisfying lack of noise. She was frustrated and needed something to clatter. "None of your business. We're not talking about me!"

"Why aren't we talking about you? What makes your life sacred? Why do we always have to talk about me and my marriage?" Janet shouted, slamming down her mug and sloshing the contents on the counter.

"Because you're the one in an abusive relationship!" Kate shouted back, her temper making her shake.

"Stop using that word!"

"I'm worried sick about you, and I can't get you to see the truth about Larry! He won't change. He needs help. And you need to get out while you can!"

"You don't understand!" Janet stomped her foot like an errant child.

"I understand that one day his *temper,* as you call it, could get you killed!"

Tears filled Janet's eyes. "I know he's not perfect, but I love him!"

The strangled quality of her sister's voice speared Kate. "And I love *you* too much to let him keep hurting you."

The dam burst, and Janet ducked her head to her hands and sobbed. "I'm scared, Katie."

Her heart wrenching, Kate hurried to her sister and pulled her into a bear hug. "I know. I'm scared for you."

Janet sniffled. "I don't want to be alone."

"You won't be. You'll always have me."

"I don't want to start over. I'd have to quit my job and leave town, or he'd never leave me be."

She was right about that much. Janet only stood a chance of truly breaking free of Larry if she started over in another town, even another state.

"I'd help you however I could. You know that." She stroked her sister's back, trying not to resent the turmoil and upheaval moving again would mean to her own life. She had begun to put down roots here after leaving her home, her friends in Ohio for Janet. And in the last few hours, during the precious hours she'd spent getting to know Gage, she'd begun thinking in terms of her own future. She wanted to find a man to love and settle down with. Start a family.

Janet is your family. Your only family right now... Guilt and loyalty jabbed her with a one-two punch.

"I know you'd help me. And I love you for that. I do. But...I just don't think I can do it, Katie. It's really not so bad most of the time. If I'd just remember not to make him so mad, everything would be fine."

Kate hugged her sister tighter, fighting back the groan of defeat when Janet went back to her same denials and blind justifications. At least this morning she'd gotten Janet to think in terms of leaving, even if just to shoot down the idea. Maybe Janet was finally beginning to come around.

Kate only prayed her sister saw the light and got away from Larry before it was too late.

A few hours later, when he took over guard duty from Bart, Gage found the senator at the large living room window that looked out on the ranch buildings and pens. Gage followed the direction of Hank's gaze and found him watching Cole at the back of a small trailer, helping unload cows into a holding area.

"So what happens with the cows now that they've been rounded up?" Gage asked.

Hank glanced at Gage as if he'd just noticed him standing beside him. "Well, that's only a fraction of the herd. The hands will be bringing the rest of them back in over the next day or two as they're located and herded back by cowboys on horseback or driven back here in trailers."

Ice cubes in the glass the senator held tinkled as he took a sip of whiskey. Gage lifted an eyebrow. The senator was starting his drinking early today. Because Cole was home?

"Once they're all back here, the cows are separated from the calves, and they're weighed and sent out to market in eighteen-wheelers."

"Payday," Gage said.

"Yep." Hank sipped again. "The whole year of ranching boils down to market day, what the herd weighs, how many he has to sell, how many calves he has. It's a tense and busy time on a ranch."

Full of distractions and chaos for the ranchers. What better time for Hank's enemies to strike at Cole's high-profile guest? Gage shifted his weight uneasily as he stared out at the activity in the holding pens. Had the tripped alarms this week been trial runs, tests of the security system?

"Senator Kelley." Hank and Gage both turned when Hannah entered the living room. "Cole asked me to include you in the breakfast I made for him this morning. I've held it in the oven if you want to eat now."

Hank seemed surprised that the housekeeper had cooked for him. "Thank you, Hannah. I'll be right in." He drained his drink then refilled the highball glass before leaving the living room. "Shall we?" he asked Gage as he headed to breakfast.

Hannah had spread a feast of ham, eggs, fried potatoes, biscuits with jelly, stewed cinnamon apples and orange juice on the table. Gage's stomach growled, despite having eaten the muffins Kate sent home with him.

"This looks terrific. Thank you," Gage told Hannah as he took a seat.

She gave Hank a surly glance before answering Gage. "Cole needed a big breakfast before he set to work. He might not get a break for lunch, and he's got a full day of hard labor ahead of him. He's the one that asked me to include the ranch guests when I cooked."

Hank's cell phone rang, and he took the call as he settled at the table. Hannah sniffed and rolled her eyes. Her disdain for Cole's father was almost humorous—except *any* animosity toward the senator couldn't be ignored. Gage sized up the short, heavyset woman. Could she be working with the senator's enemies from the inside? He couldn't ignore the idea that someone at the ranch, someone Cole trusted, could be helping the people trying to get to Hank. Just how much did Hannah dislike Hank?

Gage tucked into his breakfast while Hank talked to his assistant.

"And how are you feeling, Cindy? Everything all right with the baby?" Hank asked.

Gage glanced up from his eggs, startled by Hank's uncharacteristic concern for someone besides himself. He'd met Cindy Jensen briefly when Dylan Kelley had hired him to guard his father, and the attractive aide who worked for Hank had only barely been showing a baby bump.

"Well, take care of yourself," Hank said. "I need you on the job now more than ever. I hate being stuck up here when there's so much work to be done."

Ah. Gage frowned and dug into his food again. So Hank's concern was merely in how Cindy's health affected her ability to run his office in his absence. Maybe the senator's selfish reputation was deserved after all.

They ate in silence for several minutes before Hank said, "You look tired."

Gage shrugged. "Didn't get much sleep last night."

"Bart tells me you went out. Is bar-hopping really a good idea for a bodyguard, even in his off hours?"

Gage set his fork down, his free hand fisting on his lap. "I wasn't at a bar."

"Oh? Where'd you go then?"

He didn't really think he owed the senator any explanation of how he spent his free time, but he heard himself say, "Kate Rogers called the ranch looking for me. She asked me to come over when she thought she might have a problem with—" He stopped just short of saying *her brother-in-law.* Kate's personal business was private. "Someone who'd harassed her in the past."

"Stayed all night, did you? No sleep?" Hank gave him a lecherous grin.

Gage gritted his teeth and the biscuit in his hand crumbled under his grip. "Watch it, old man. Kate's not that kind of woman."

Hank chuckled and hummed a glib, "Mm-hm."

Gage started to defend his actions and Kate's reputation with further explanations, but a memory of the soul-branding kiss he'd shared with Kate before leaving her house taunted him. If Kate wasn't that kind of woman, why had he put the moves on her the way he had? Sure, he'd felt a spark of attraction from her, but knowing she shared a physical interest in him didn't mean he had to act on it. He didn't want Kate to think he didn't respect what he assumed were her views on premarital sex.

And a sexual fling was just the kind of distraction that he didn't need while he protected a U.S. Senator.

A sexual fling...

Kate naked, wrapped around him, kissing him with the

sweet honesty and pure emotion she'd had this morning…her petite body tucked beneath his…her sky-blue eyes shining at him with a fiery passion….

His mouth suddenly going dry, Gage reached for his orange juice with a shaky hand. He drank deeply, emptying the glass, but still felt parched. Guilt shimmied through him. In light of Kate's deeply held beliefs, even imagining her in the throes of hot sex felt wrong. He could not, would not ask Kate to compromise her convictions, no matter how badly he wanted her. He respected her too much to put her in that position.

"…head outside to watch the sorting."

Gage snapped his attention to Hank, realizing he'd missed most of what the senator had said. "I'm sorry. What?"

"You know I'm bored out of my gourd if sorting cows passes for a morning's entertainment, but I don't relish sitting around inside all day either." Hank pushed his plate away and dropped his napkin on the table.

"Can't you watch from the window?" Gage wiped his mouth and pushed his chair back. "You're safer inside."

Hank blew him off with a buzz of his lips and a waved hand. "I'll be fine. Who's going to get me with you and all those ranch hands around?"

And what if one of the ranch hands is working with Hank's enemies?

"You'd still be vulnerable. If you keep ignoring my advice and Bart's, we can't guarantee your saf—"

"Then you're fired. I didn't ask for a bodyguard. Hiring you was Dylan's idea." Hank polished off his second glass of Maker's Mark and scooted back from the table.

"Exactly. He hired me, and only he can fire me. So you're stuck with me, for better or worse." Gage followed Hank to the front door where the senator took his coat from the rack and shoved his arms in the sleeves. "Senator, you need to stay—"

"Can it, Prescott. I'm old enough to be your father, and I won't have you telling me what I can and can't do. Just do your job, and I'll be fine. But I'm going outside."

Even if that meant putting Gage, Cole and the other ranch hands at greater risk with his presence. Gage sighed heavily and grabbed his coat as he followed the hardheaded and selfish senator into the cool October morning.

Hank sauntered across the dry ranch yard toward the holding pen where a handful of cowboys worked with Cole getting the calves sorted from the adults and herded onto a contained platform where they could be weighed.

"Morning, gentlemen," the senator greeted cheerfully in his best politician's voice.

Cole glanced toward his father but said nothing.

Gage stepped up to the fence beside Hank and rested his arms on the top bar, watching the cowboys in action. In the pen, he recognized the ranch manager, Rusty Moore, at the chute, Ben from the stable atop Blaze, and Kenny Greene— the younger hand that he and the sheriff had caught behind the barn on the night trespassers had cut the fence in the lower pasture. The young hand noticed Gage and hesitated in his work, staring back at Gage with a startled expression.

When Kenny got a face full of dirt as a large bull near him bucked, Cole shouted, "Hey, cowboy, pay attention! You start daydreaming in there with those cattle, and you could be killed."

"Sorry, boss." Kenny got back to work, waving a tool that looked like a giant fly-swatter at a cow to steer it away from the chute.

Cole rode up to the fence where Gage and Hank stood observing. Reining in his horse, he knocked his hat back to wipe grime and sweat from his brow. "Senator," he said formally, "there something I can do for you?"

The stiff form of address Cole used for his father resounded in Gage's head, and he heard Kate saying, *I don't think the senator was a very good father.*

Hank flashed his son a nervous-looking smile. "Just watching. Brings back a lot of memories."

Cole gave his father a skeptical frown. "You hated ranching. Uncle Donald said you couldn't leave Montana fast enough."

"True enough. I didn't want to make a career of ranching, but that doesn't mean all my memories of the family business are bad."

Cole made no reply.

Gage shifted his weight from one foot to the other, uncomfortable being in the vicinity of the family tension. He thought of Janet's snarky comments to Kate that morning and wondered how the bonds of family could be so strong for some people when the relationships were strained and acrimonious. He knew, in Kate's case, her optimism, forgiving nature and experience with the Zooks gave her hope that her relationship with Janet could be close and loving.

Gage ground his back teeth together in frustration. From what he'd seen, Janet used Kate's optimism as a weapon, exploiting her sister's good nature and taking advantage of her forgiveness. He tried to tell himself the sisters' relationship was none of his business, but he'd grown to care deeply for Kate and hated seeing her mistreated.

"So how is your Uncle Donald?" Hank asked after an awkward moment of silence passed.

Gage searched his memory of the file he'd read on the Kelley family before taking the assignment to protect Hank. Donald Kelley, the senator's half-brother, lived in another small town near Maple Cove, and ran a successful chain of barbecue restaurants. Donald had helped raise Cole when he'd left California as a teenager.

"Why don't you call him yourself and ask?" Cole returned, his attention focused on the activity in the pen.

The muscles in Hank's jaw tightened, and he sent his son a glower of exasperation. "Maybe I will," he shot back tightly.

Then, taking a deep breath, Hank scratched his chin and said more calmly, "I...could help with the sorting if you wanted. I still know how to rope."

Gage jerked his gaze toward Hank. "What?"

This was the first he'd heard of the senator's intentions. Was this a play to get back in his son's good graces? Gage shifted his attention to the thousand-pound animals thundering through the corral, bumping and jostling each other in the tight confines, then he glanced at Cole. How was he supposed to protect the senator from a mishap in that chaos?

Cole stared at his father suspiciously, and Gage had opened his mouth to object when Cole said, "When's the last time you had a drink?"

Hank stepped back from the fence and shoved his hands in his pockets. "I...well, what difference does that make?"

"I won't have anyone in here working that isn't fully cognizant and in control." Cole shoved his hat back in place. "I know how you love your Maker's Mark, so I have to be sure."

"I'm fine," Hank said.

Gage grunted and kicked the dirt. "Sir, you had two drinks with your breakfast."

The senator shot him a dirty look. "Yes, with *food!* I'm fine." He held his hand out to Cole. "Steady as a rock."

Cole shook his head. "Not this time." He hesitated, then said, "But skip the booze tomorrow, and we'll talk." He turned as if to ride away and get back to work but paused, shifting his attention to Gage. "Say, Prescott, where were you coming in from this morning at the crack of dawn when I was heading out to start work?"

Standing straighter, Gage prepared to tell the rancher to

mind his own business, when he saw the glint of mischief and tug of a grin on Cole's face. Gage arched one eyebrow. "Christmas shopping."

Hank scoffed. "Christmas shopping, my eye," he grumbled, then louder to Cole, "He was at his girlfriend's house."

"Girlfriend?" Cole repeated, clearly surprised.

Gage shot Hank a quelling look which went ignored.

"Yeah, he was hitting on that pretty waitress at the diner in town last week."

"I wasn't hitting on her," Gage said, realizing too late that his objection was as good as admitting guilt.

"At the diner? You mean Kate Rogers?" Cole asked, his expression surprised.

Hank gave Gage a smug look. Payback. "I think that's her name. Pretty little blonde. She made a box of pastries especially for him."

They had Ben's attention now, and the ranch hand gaped at Gage. "You're dating Kate Rogers? You asked her out, and she actually said *yes?*"

Gage raised a hand and shook his head. "I didn't say that."

"But that is where you said you were all night last night. At her house? Am I right?" Hank prodded.

Gage clenched his teeth. If he hadn't sworn to protect the senator's life, Gage would have killed Hank himself.

"I'll be danged." Ben snorted and sauntered away, shaking his head.

Cole chuckled. "You dog. Do you have any idea how many cowboys have asked her out and been turned down? And you come in here and have her making you pastries inside of a week." He doffed his hat and nodded to Gage. "My hat's off to you, friend."

"It's not like that," Gage started, uncomfortable both with the attention and the direction of the conversation, but he caught himself.

Who was he kidding? He had kissed her last night. He wanted to see her again. In fact, he wanted much more from her than just a casual friendship or a meaningless fling. So why *hadn't* he asked her out?

Cole's expression grew more serious, and he narrowed a sharp gaze on Gage. "Just you be sure you don't hurt her, you hear? Kate's a sweetheart, and she deserves better than a broken heart from some womanizer who's just passing through town." With that, he rode back into the fray of ranch hands, cows and flying dirt.

The rancher's warning wasn't anything he hadn't told himself. The last thing he wanted was to lead Kate on, give her false hope.

Sure, he wanted to explore a relationship with her. She was beautiful and kind, warm and funny. But she didn't need him and his black guilt and nightmares of war to drag her down. She'd be better off with someone settled and reliable, like Cole.

Gage imagined Kate with the handsome rancher and jealousy kicked him hard in the gut.

Do you have any idea how many cowboys have asked her out and been turned down? Yet she'd asked him to come to her house last night, had been kissing him this morning. So maybe exploring the chemistry he felt with Kate wasn't so preposterous. If nothing else, he wanted an opportunity to talk to Kate about Janet. Gage kicked the dry dirt at his feet and shoved his hands in his pockets. One dinner out with Kate couldn't hurt, but that was where he had to draw the line. Beyond a meal out on the town, he had nothing to offer a woman like Kate, and he couldn't live with himself if he did anything to hurt her.

Chapter 9

After watching Cole sort and weigh the cows for about an hour, Hank grew restless and went back inside to channel surf and gauge how much of the brouhaha over his numerous mistresses had died down. Having had little sleep last night, Gage found his eyes drifting closed from time to time, especially when Hank settled on the Weather Channel as he took another call from Cindy Jensen.

"Have I had any calls from Rick Garrison?" Hank asked his assistant, and the name pulled Gage out of the sleepy fog he'd drifted into. Garrison...the mercenary Hank had sent after his daughter.

"I haven't heard anything, and I'm getting...well, worried." Hank prowled the living room like a caged tiger. Not that Gage could blame him. The tedium of this assignment was making him claustrophobic, too. "Give him this number if he calls. Yes."

Gage heard the kitchen door open, heard Cole speak

warmly to the old dog, Ace, then heard footsteps as the rancher entered the living room.

Hannah appeared from the back of the house, folding a towel, and gave her boss a frown of concern. "Is something wrong, Cole?"

"Nah. Just getting something from my room." Cole glanced at the television, which still had the Weather Channel playing softly, and paused.

"Can I get you something to eat while you're in?" Hannah asked, setting the towel aside.

Cole frowned at the TV then glanced at the housekeeper. "Huh? Oh, no. I don't have time. But thanks."

Hank's conversation with his assistant continued to drone from the far side of the large room, and Gage wondered if Cole might be waiting to speak to his father.

"Are you sure there's nothing wrong, honey? You look upset." Hannah stepped closer to Cole and placed a weathered hand on his arm.

Honey? The housekeeper's warmth and motherly concern for Cole was sure a departure from the gruff manner she used toward Hank and his bodyguards. Gage suppressed a grin of amusement. Guess he knew where the older woman's loyalties lay.

"Nothing you need to worry about," Cole told Hannah, then pointed toward the TV where the ten-day forecast for the area around Maple Cove glowed on the screen. "Unless you can do something to stop this front that's moving in. That's gonna screw things up for me. Big time."

"How so?" Gage asked.

"Well, I just got word that part of the herd, the part I was expecting to be brought in today, has about a hundred head missing. They're lost somewhere up in the mountains apparently, and we're gonna need extra time and manpower to find 'em and bring 'em in."

"And this front will prevent that from happening some-how?" Gage asked.

Cole sighed, then explained patiently, "I've had trucks—eighteen-wheelers—scheduled for months to take my herd to market tomorrow. But with more than half of the cows still out and one hundred head missing until God knows when, I'm gonna have to cancel the trucks and reschedule. There's no telling when I can get the trucks in here now. Other ranchers will have dibs on the rigs for the next week or so, I'm sure, and now there's this front coming," he waved a hand toward the TV and furrowed his brow, "that could dump snow on the road and bury the fields."

"Don't they plow the roads around here?" Gage asked.

"The main roads, but not some of the smaller roads to get up here. Thing is, if the field's under snow, the cows can't get to the hay stubble I'd need them to eat to keep their weight while we wait on the trucks." Cole rubbed the back of his neck and blew out another frustrated sigh.

Gage couldn't imagine the stress these complications put on Cole. The outcome of the whole ranching season boiled down to just a few days, and Cole's profit or loss for the year was at the mercy of factors out of his hands.

"Can I do anything?" Hannah asked.

Cole squeezed the housekeeper's shoulder as he headed out of the room. "Pray."

Hannah smiled at the young rancher. "I already do. For you. Every day."

Across the room, Hank snapped his cell phone closed and grumbled, "My life has turned to crap."

Hannah retrieved the discarded towel and squared her shoulders as she turned to leave, muttering, "Seems about right."

Gage frowned and settled back in the sofa cushions. Had Hank heard anything his son had just said about the precarious position he was in with getting his herd to market? Gage hated to think the senator was really so self-absorbed, so unconcerned about the trouble his son was facing that he could be complaining about his own life just seconds after Cole's explanation of the hurdles he was facing.

"What are you fixing for lunch?" Hank called to Hannah before she disappeared into the laundry room.

"For you? Nothing," came the brisk reply.

Hank glowered at the doorway where Hannah had exited, then faced Gage. "Looks like we're going into town to eat." He gave a humorless chuckle. "Lucky you. You get to see your girlfriend at the diner again."

Gage swallowed the urge to respond to the senator's comment, even to tell him today was Kate's day off. What was the point?

Within minutes, Hank had his coat on and was waiting impatiently by the door for Gage to drive him to town. Gage ruffled Ace's fur as he walked out to the senator's Town Car and earned a tail wag and a lick on the hand. When Ace started toward Hank, Gage caught the old dog's collar and squatted beside him. "He's not a dog person, remember, boy?"

With a last pat for Ace, Gage climbed behind the steering wheel and headed into Maple Cove. The diner was bustling as usual but still felt empty to Gage without Kate there. Laurie Emerson, their waitress from last week, was working again today, and she smiled warmly when she recognized the senator.

"Senator Kelley, I didn't know you were still in town." Laurie handed Hank and Gage each a menu. "Are you enjoying your vacation here in Maple Cove?"

"It's not a vacation," Hank said flatly, before apparently realizing he should be in politician mode and plastering a toothy grin on his face. "But the town is just as beautiful and friendly as I remember from my youth, thank you. Maybe when I do get some time off, I'll come back to do some fly-fishing."

"Oh, yes! My husband loves to fly-fish in the Yellowstone and Boulder rivers. I tell you, Paradise Valley has the best fly-fishing anywhere." She grinned and nudged Hank's shoulder. "But then you'd know that, having grown up here, huh?"

While Laurie took Hank's order, Gage stole away from the table long enough to catch Janet at the counter. "Was everything all right when you got home this morning? Any problems with Larry?"

Janet glared at him as she started a fresh pot of coffee brewing. "Everything was fine. No thanks to you."

"Me?" Gage leaned on the lunch counter and arched an eyebrow in query.

"Larry says you threatened him."

Gage pitched his voice low for Janet's ears only. "Someone needs to stand up to him, tell him he can't get away with beating you."

"I don't know what Kate's been telling you, but I don't need your help. I'm fine. So back off." She wadded the trash from the coffee pot and tossed it in the wastebasket.

"Kate's worried about you. And frankly, so am I. Larry's not going to change until he gets counseling, if then. You need to get out while you can."

Janet scowled at him. "My marriage is none of your business. I already have to leave work early today to appease Larry. He thinks on the days I work late at the diner I'm meeting someone. After finding out you were at Kate's at the same time I was last night, he's demanded I be home to make his supper and stay in with him tonight."

"You see? He's got you changing your life and jumping through hoops to cater to his baseless jealousy. Who's going to work the dinner shift if you don't?"

"Kate, of course."

"Today is her day off."

"I explained the situation, and she agreed to come in for me tonight."

Gage gritted his teeth. "She works two jobs here already and needs time to rest and relax."

"And I'm her only sister and needed a favor. When your family needs you, that comes first." Janet looked a tad smug to Gage. As if she knew she had a trump card with Kate because of her views on family.

"When's the last time you did Kate any favors?" Gage said, his voice tight with irritation.

Stay out of this. Their family dynamic is not your job. Don't get distracted.

But he'd come to care about Kate and that *did* make her his business.

Janet pulled her eyebrows into a frown. "I do her favors."

"When? You ever work an extra shift so she could get some well-deserved time off? Have you ever uprooted your whole life to be close to her and help her with a difficult marriage?"

Janet's chin hitched up. "Butt out, Gage."

Butting out might be exactly what he should do, but he couldn't stand to see Janet take advantage of Kate. "This Thursday night, you're going to offer to work Kate's shift so she can have the night off. Got it?"

Janet scoffed. "What makes you think so?"

"Because I'm going to ask her to dinner that night, and you owe her that much and more."

He hadn't known until the words left his mouth that he'd decided to ask Kate out. Who knew how long he'd be in town and what would come of their relationship? Starting up a relationship with someone as sweet and vulnerable to heartache as Kate was dangerous. And yet...the time for second-guessing had passed. Because last night he *had* started something with Kate. Now he could only pray his association with her didn't destroy the innocence and inner beauty he found so irresistible in her.

"There you go, darlin'," Hank said, handing Laurie Emerson a hundred dollar bill with his lunch ticket. "Keep the change."

Laurie's face lit when she saw the denomination of the bill he'd given her. "Oh, my! Thank you, Senator! And you have a nice day."

He gave her a wink and smile, and the waitress practically swooned.

Gage suppressed a groan. Women were popping up across the country claiming adulterous affairs with the married man, trashing his reputation as a family-values politician, and still the man flirted shamelessly with every attractive woman he met.

Hank strolled toward the diner door, then waited for Gage to check the sidewalk and open the Town Car door for him before leaving the relative safety of the diner. At least he was partially following Gage's instructions now.

As soon as they were on the road, headed back to the Bar Lazy K, Hank had his cell phone out, calling his assistant. "Have you gotten in touch with Rick Garrison yet?"

Gage assumed from the terse curse word Hank muttered under his breath that the reply was a negative.

"Well, when you do reach him, tell him he doesn't see another penny of his fee until I have proof Lana is safe. And call Senator Goldsmith and reschedule next week's lunch. Clearly this situation with…you know what…is going to take longer to clear up than I'd thought. I'll probably be stuck up here a few more weeks."

Gage couldn't help the lift in his spirits at the thought of staying in Montana, close to Kate, for the next several weeks.

A smile twitched at his lips as anticipation of seeing her again filled his chest like a balloon.

"No. I don't want to do any interviews until this mess with all those women blows over. Not even by phone. Continue to tell them I've said all I have to say on the matter and have no further comment at this time."

Wham!

Gage's head snapped forward as the Town Car was rammed from behind. His gaze jerked to the rearview mirror. Where had that truck come from?

Hank barked, "What the—!"

Bam!

Sweat popped out on Gage's lip. The dark blue truck was intentionally ramming them! He reached with one hand under his jacket for his weapon and steered the Town Car along the two-lane highway with the other. "Get on the floor!"

With a roar of its motor, the pickup truck sped around them. The muzzle of a rifle appeared out the passenger window—aimed at the backseat.

"Stay down!" Gage shouted.

"Who is—"

Crack! Thunk.

The rifle kicked up as it was fired, and the bullet hit the side of the Town Car.

Gage lowered the driver's window a couple of inches and squeezed off two rounds. Adrenaline pumped through him, but he kept a steady hand.

Squealing tires, the truck sped away.

"Senator, are you all right?" Gage slowed to a stop, pulling off the road and giving the area an encompassing glance. Other than the retreating pickup, they were alone on the rural highway.

"I— Yes." Hank pushed up from the floor, looking dazed but clearly unhurt. "Where did they come from? There's...there's nowhere to hide out here." He waved a hand to the sprawling landscape with miles of unimpeded visibility.

Recriminations lashed Gage. He'd been thinking about Kate, not keeping a watchful eye on other vehicles on the road. Even if a large pickup like the one that had attacked them was a common sight in Montana, he should have been more alert to the truck's approach. Damn it!

Hank brushed imagined dirt off his shirt as he settled on the back seat again. He narrowed a glare on Gage. "Why didn't you see them following us?"

Gage's temper spiked, fueled by adrenaline, guilt and frustration. "And why won't you level with me? I'm having a hard enough time keeping you safe when you don't obey my instructions, but when you won't tell me who I'm protecting you from, what the threat is, why someone wants to hurt you, I'm working blind!"

Hank sat taller and met Gage's glare evenly. "I can't tell you. My hands are tied. I was warned that if I said anything to anyone, I'd be destroyed."

"And yet they seem to be gunning for you regardless of what you have or haven't told me." Gage hitched a thumb in the direction the truck had gone. He clenched his teeth so hard his molars hurt. "Now start talking. Who has threatened you?"

Hank only stared at him for long seconds.

"They've already taken your daughter hostage and shot at you. How much more danger are you going to put the people around you in before you do something to stop them?"

"I'm handling them my own way."

"With your mercenary? He hasn't been in touch in days. What does that tell you?" Gage shifted closer to Hank and lowered his voice. "Who has threatened you? And why?"

The senator turned his gaze out the window, his jaw tight. "My political enemies."

"Be more specific."

Hank sighed and dropped his chin to his chest. "They call themselves the Raven's Head Society. They're a highly secret organization of businessmen, financial leaders, lobbyists and high-powered statesmen who are working through nefarious means to push their own political agenda."

"How do you know about them if they're so secretive?"

"I was invited to a meeting. When I saw what they were about, I wanted out, but—"

"But?"

"They've threatened me, warned me not to tell anyone what they're planning. They...want me to take the fall for their scheme."

A tingle nipped Gage's spine. "And what are they planning?"

Hank shook his head. "I can't tell you. I...shouldn't have said that much. They took Lana to force my hand. They want me to do...things...illegal things to promote their agenda and—"

"Who are they? Name names."

Hank sent Gage an incredulous look. "Are you insane? If I started naming names, I'd be as good as dead!"

"Ernie Bradshaw? The owner of that insurance company?"

Hank paled. "How did you—"

"That's whose cabin Lana indicated she was being held at. If his cabin is involved in her kidnapping, it stands to reason he's part of this Raven's Head Society."

Hank rolled his shoulders and huffed an irritated sigh. "Yeah, I think he's involved."

"Who else?"

The senator shook his head. "No. You know enough to protect me. I won't say any more. But understand this...these people are well-connected and have access to a great deal of money. They could hire people to do their dirty work while they sit back and pull the strings."

Gage chewed his bottom lip, considering the facts. "If that's the case, the people in that truck were probably local yahoos bought off to take a potshot at you."

"It was a warning, I'm sure," Hank leaned his head back, his expression pure misery. "So far, I've refused to cooperate with them…except that I haven't called the police or brought in the FBI. They were very clear that Lana would die and my career would be ruined if I talked to the authorities."

"How would they know if you talked to the FBI?"

"Hell, they could have people planted in the FBI for all I know!" A vein at Hank's temple pulsed as he shouted. "These are powerful, dangerous people we're talking about!"

Gage swiped a hand over his mouth. Acid churned in his gut. This assignment was bigger and more complex than he'd had any idea. "You need to tell Cole."

Hank's eyes widened. "No!"

"You're staying at his ranch, putting him and his employees in the line of fire. He has a right to know what's at stake."

Shaking his head, the senator held up a hand. "He's got enough to worry about with his lost cows and the bad weather coming and—no."

So Hank *had* been listening to his son earlier…

"The Society was very clear. I can't tell Cole. His life would be at risk, as Lana's already is." Deep creases formed beside Hank's eyes and mouth. "I haven't been there for my family the way I should have been over the years, but…I love them. I won't do anything to put them at risk."

"Anything *else,* you mean. Aren't they already at risk because of the choices you've made?" Gage knew he'd crossed a line, but he needed Hank to stop dancing around certain truths and be completely up front.

Hank flinched as if taking a physical blow.

"Look," Gage said, raking fingers through his hair, "Things are going to be different from here on out. Clearly these people know where you are. You *will* listen to me and follow my directives. You will stay at the ranch, inside, away from windows, where you are better protected."

Hank's scowl let Gage know how his ultimatum was being received.

"No more lunches in town." Gage took solace in the fact he still had nights off and could see Kate in the evenings, if not at lunch. "You will not use your cell any longer."

"Wha—!"

"If you have to make phone calls, we'll get you a phone with a secure line."

The senator glared out the window and grumbled under his breath.

"Do you want my protection or not?"

Hank sent Gage a quick churlish glance. "Yes. I just hate being a prisoner like this."

Gage resisted the temptation to point out that Cole's luxury ranch house was a far cry from a prison. "Those are my terms going forward. Do we have an understanding?"

Hank closed his eyes, and his shoulders drooped. "We do."

Chapter 10

When they returned to the Bar Lazy K Ranch, Gage filled Bart in on the attack and the new understanding he and Hank had reached. Hank chafed under the new rules, insisting that he had to use his cell to be in touch with his assistant on business.

Finally, Bart told Gage he'd start his shift early so that Gage could go into Livingston to arrange for a cell with a secure line. As he made the short trip to the nearby city, Gage's mind wandered frequently to Kate and how she was likely spending her day off. Had she given much thought to their kiss? Was she regretting it? Anticipating seeing him again?

He'd told Janet he was going to ask Kate out for Thursday night, just two nights away, so, good to his word, he stopped by Kate's house on his way back to the ranch.

"Gage?" Kate's face reflected surprise then delight when

she answered the door. "To what do I owe this honor?" She opened her door wider and stood back to let him in.

"I was in the neighborhood and thought I'd stop by."

She tipped her head and gave him a skeptical look. "In the neighborhood? Really?"

He grinned. "Well, yeah. I was in the neighborhood, because I wanted to see you, wanted to ask you to go to dinner with me on Thursday."

"Oh, I see." She chuckled, then sobered and blinked at him as if she'd just realized what he'd said. "Wait, you're asking me out? On a date?"

"That's what they call it where I come from." He quirked an insouciant grin that belied the nervous patter in his chest. Geez, he felt thirteen again, asking Carol what's-her-name to the Valentine's dance. When was the last time he'd cared enough about a woman to ask her out? When was the last time he'd been in a position to actually take a woman on a date? Months...years...since before he'd been deployed to Afghanistan.

He drew a slow deep breath, hoping to calm his schoolboy jitters. Her answer mattered a great deal to him. Maybe too much. He wasn't supposed to care this much about a woman if he was going to keep his head in the game protecting the senator.

"I'm supposed to work on Thursday." Kate wet her lips and took a seat on her couch, next to her fluffball cat.

Sinatra. That was his name. Gage settled on the other side of the cat and gave the feline's soft fur a tentative stroke. He'd never been a cat person, but Sinatra seemed pretty easygoing.

"At lunch today, I took the liberty of asking Janet to cover for you. You should be all set."

Kate blinked, lifting her eyebrows, and Gage worried that he'd overstepped his bounds.

"And Janet agreed to cover for me? Really?"

"You sound surprised."

"I guess I am a bit. Janet isn't usually so obliging about working extra shifts." Kate flopped back on the cushions and gave him a suspicious look.

"Which is one of the things I'd like to talk with you about when we have dinner."

Her mouth curled up at one corner. "I haven't said yes."

Gage snapped his mouth shut and rubbed a hand on the leg of his jeans. "Oh."

"Yet."

He arched an eyebrow. "And?"

She hesitated, giving him a coy grin as she scratched Sinatra behind the ears. Soon the cat hopped down from the sofa and strolled toward the kitchen. Kate took advantage of the vacated space on the couch and scooted closer to Gage. "What time would you like to pick me up?"

He buried his hand in her silky hair and pulled her close for a kiss. "How does six sound?"

Gage left Kate's place after sharing dinner and several more heated kisses with her. As he drove away from her house, he realized he was wearing a sappy grin. Kate, her sunny optimism and enjoyment of life's simple pleasures, was rubbing off on him. He found himself savoring the sunset, humming with the radio and, mostly, anticipating his date with Kate on Thursday night. Deciding he'd better ensure Janet's cooperation, he swung by the diner on his way back to the ranch.

He sat at the counter and enjoyed a piece of Kate's apple pie while Janet helped other customers. When she came by to clear away his plate and leave his bill, he caught her wrist before she could hustle off to the kitchen. "Do I have your word that you'll cover for Kate Thursday?"

Janet rolled her eyes. "Maybe. I'll see."

"Not good enough. Our plans are set. I need your word." When Janet hesitated, he asked, "Do you love your sister?"

She looked affronted by the question. "Of course! That's not the issue."

"How many favors has Kate done for you just this week? Huh?"

Janet's expression grew contrite, and she pursed up her mouth in acquiescence. "Fine. I'll try."

"Good." Gage slid more than enough money to cover the pie and a generous tip across the counter, then shoved his arms in his jacket. Only vaguely certain Janet would uphold her promise, Gage left the diner and started up the starlit town street toward Rusty's truck. Maple Cove was deserted, the stores all dark inside, and he remembered what Kate had told him about the local ranchers not staying out late due to their early-morning hours.

With the sun down, the temperature had taken a nosedive, and Gage rubbed his hands together, buffing the chill from them. He'd have to see about getting a warm pair of gloves if he was going to be staying in Montana with the senator much longer.

Perhaps Cole could—

Wham! A hard object struck his head from behind. Pain blasted through his skull as he stumbled to catch his balance.

"Threaten me, will you?" a voice growled from the alley beside him.

Blinking off the stars that danced in his vision, Gage spun to face his attacker. Larry stood in the shadows of the alley, a broken tree limb in his hand. "I told you to stay away from my wife."

"And you should learn to trust Janet if you love her." Gage touched the back of his head searching for any bleeding. Pain throbbed under his fingers.

Larry lurched toward him again, swinging the branch in an arcing motion.

Gage ducked, avoiding the blow.

"I saw you in there with her! I saw your cozy conversation." Spittle flew from Larry's mouth, and his eyes were wide and wild. He swung again, and though Gage dodged to get out of the way, he caught a glancing blow on the shoulder.

"What were you two talking about?"

Gage sighed, holding out his hands in a conciliatory gesture. He could kick Larry's butt ten ways to Tuesday, but he knew Kate would disapprove, so he opted for appeasement and diffusing Larry's wrath. "I asked her to cover for Kate on Thursday, so we could go to dinner together."

"Kate?"

"Yeah, Kate. She's the one I'm interested in. I don't steal other people's wives."

Larry shifted his weight and swapped the branch from one hand to the other. "I don't believe you. Kate's not even working tonight. Why would you stop in if she's not there?"

He met Larry's skeptical glare calmly, pushing down the twinges of frustration and contempt for this man who hit his wife. "A guy's gotta eat."

"You were telling her to leave me, weren't you?" Larry growled, his eyes narrowing further.

Gage said nothing. The truth would only provoke Larry.

Correctly taking Gage's silence as confirmation, Larry swung the branch again and called Gage a vile name.

Gage caught the branch and jerked it from Larry's hands.

Shaking with rage, Larry assumed a fighting stance, fists raised. "You and Kate are in it together. That bitch sister of Janet's is always talking trash about me!"

Hearing the derogatory term he called Kate, Gage's temper skyrocketed. He surged forward, jamming his nose close to Larry's and planting his hands in the man's chest with a hard shove. "Maybe that's because it's the truth. Only cowardly scum has to beat up a woman to feel like a man."

Larry rocked his head forward and butted Gage's face with his head. Pain streaked from his nose through his sinuses, and reacting purely on instinct, Gage swung a fist that caught Larry in the jaw. After staggering back a step, Larry lowered his head and charged at Gage, catching him the gut and shoving him back several steps before they crashed into the brick wall of the alley.

Gage wrapped his arm around Larry's neck, shoving his head down and immobilizing him in a wrestler's hold. "I could break your neck with one twist, pal. You don't want to get into it with me. You won't win."

Larry was breathing hard, and blood dripped from his split lip. "Let go of me, you freak!"

"I will on two conditions."

Janet's husband struggled to get free of his grip, and Gage tweaked his grip just enough for Larry to yelp in pain and stop squirming.

"First, you're never going to disrespect Kate like that again. Ever. And second, you're not going to say anything to Janet about her taking the late shift on Thursday night. She's working Kate's shift as payback for all the favors Kate's done Janet. No jealous rages or guilt trips. Got it?"

Larry grunted weakly and wheezed a breath. Releasing him, Gage gave the man a shove and aimed a finger at him. "Stay away from me, or next time I might not be so lenient. I'd love nothing better than to give you a taste of your own medicine, you wife-beating scum bag."

Larry leveled a malevolent glare on him as Gage backed toward the street. Only after he had reached Rusty's truck did he finger the knot on his head and test his nose for damage. He'd have a goose egg on the back of his head and a bruised nose, but he didn't think anything was broken. The bouncy ride home over potholed rural roads and with the truck's aged shock absorbers left Gage with a throbbing headache by the time he reached the ranch.

As he headed to the guest quarters in the main house, a disturbing thought occurred to him. Could any of the trouble at the ranch or the shooter on the road today have been directed at him instead of Hank? Could any of the incidents have been Larry striking out at what he perceived to be a threat to his marriage?

As unlikely as it seemed, he couldn't discount the possibility. Especially in light of tonight's attack.

On Wednesday, in accordance with the new understanding he'd reached with Hank, Gage and the senator kept a low profile at the ranch. They watched a lot of television, frequently flipping channels to monitor the progress of the coming cold front that threatened snow, and Hank used his new secure phone to confer with his assistant. Gage welcomed the quiet time, since his head hurt like crazy. His hair covered the knot on his head and the external swelling told him he probably didn't have a concussion. He did have a dark shadow across the bridge of his nose, though, a clear sign he'd been in a brawl the night before.

When Cole came in to check the weather forecast and grab a bite of lunch, he took one look at Gage and raised an eyebrow. "So...what did the other guy look like when you finished with him?"

Gage peered over the edge of his coffee mug and grunted. "Better than he could have. But I knew how his sister-in-law would feel about me rearranging his face, so..." He shrugged.

Cole flashed a wry grin. "You need anything? Aspirin? Ice?"

Gage shook his head and instantly regretted it. "I found some Tylenol. I'll live."

Cole gave the Weather Channel one last disgruntled glance, then headed back out to the stock pens with a sandwich in one hand and a cup of coffee in the other.

That evening after he got off duty, Gage took a walk on the property to stretch his legs and get a bit of fresh air. Staying cooped up inside made him as restless as it made Hank. As he passed the stable, he spotted Rusty grooming a chestnut mare and crooning softly to the horse.

Rusty turned when he heard Gage approach. "Evening, Mr. Prescott. Everything all right up at the house?"

"For the time being." Gage stroked the mare's nose, and the horse nickered gently in response. "Thanks again for loaning me your truck. I was hoping to use it again tomorrow night if you don't mind."

The older man waved a hand in dismissal. "No problem. I'll be heading out on Red at some point tomorrow to look for those lost cows. So the truck's all yours."

Gage watched the Native American manager rub down his horse's back with a towel and shuffle over to put away the curry comb he'd been using. "How likely is it Cole will be able to find those lost cows and get the herd off to market before that storm hits?"

Rusty chuckled. "If sheer determination and stubbornness have anything to do with it, you can bet he'll pull it off."

"And realistically speaking?"

Ace wandered into the stable and sat down at Rusty's feet with a whine for attention. Rusty gave the old dog's head a pat. "It'll be a feat to get it all done. But Cole's one of the best ranchers I've ever had the honor to work for. If anyone can do it, he can." He walked back to his horse and led the mare into an empty stall. "So you mustered up the nerve to ask Kate Rogers out, huh?"

Gage furrowed his brow. "Who told you that?"

The older man grinned. "No one. I just figured if you're

planning ahead to need my truck tomorrow, it had to be for a special reason. No better reason than a woman. Based on what I heard you telling Cole the other morning by the sorting pen, I filled in the blank."

Gage gave the ranch manager a grin. "Not bad."

Rusty finished settling Red in for the night and hitched his head, telling Gage to follow him as he walked out of the stable. "I also figure that ornery Larry Henderson is responsible for turning your nose black and blue."

Gage shoved his hands in his back pockets as he strolled toward the bunkhouse with Rusty. "How'd you guess?"

"Just connected the dots. Everyone know Larry's got the temper of a rattlesnake."

Gage frowned. "So why doesn't anyone do something about him?"

"A few folks have tried. He's spent a few nights in jail over the years." Rusty sighed and shook his head. "I know you want to rush in and save Kate and her sister from the jerk, but…be careful. Family situations can be a powder keg of emotions. If you push too hard, the whole mess could explode in your face."

Rusty's warning sent an uneasy tremor though Gage. As much as he wanted to help Kate, wanted to see Janet save herself, he was just passing through town, passing through their lives. He didn't need to make things worse for either sister by poking a hornets' nest. Nor could he walk away, knowing the injustice of Larry's treatment of Janet.

He nodded his acknowledgment of the advice to Rusty and told the older man goodnight. Ace followed Gage as he walked back to the main house, and before he went inside, he crouched by the old dog to scratch him behind the ears.

"I don't want to make things worse for Kate or Janet, but how am I supposed to turn a blind eye to what I see happening?" he asked the dog.

Ace yawned and gave a short whine.

"You don't."

Hearing the unexpected voice, Gage whipped around and nearly lost his balance. Hannah Brown stood by the back door watching him, a dog bowl in her hand. "Ignoring a bad situation won't make it go away. If you care about someone, you protect them. Even if it hurts them to hear the truth."

Having said her piece, she patted her leg, and Ace trotted over to her. She set the bowl on the ground and ruffled Ace's fur before disappearing inside again.

Gage sighed as he dusted dog hair from his hands and turned his gaze up to the star-filled sky. In less than twenty-four hours, he'd be picking Kate up for their date. He had one day to decide whether to take Hannah's advice or heed Rusty's warning.

Chapter 11

As he parked at the curb in front of Kate's house the next evening, Gage still felt uneasy about his plan to have a frank discussion with Kate about her sister. Rusty's dire prediction that Gage's meddling could backfire hovered over him like a black cloud.

His knock on Kate's front door was answered promptly. Kate took one look at his bruised face, and her welcoming smile morphed into an expression of dismay. "What happened to you?"

"Larry happened."

Her brow puckered. "Larry?"

"He saw me talking to Janet at the diner the other night when I stopped in for dessert and assumed I was hitting on her."

Kate's shoulders sagged, and she closed her eyes with a defeated sigh. "Oh, no."

Gage stood back and hitched his head toward Rusty's truck. "Ready to go?"

She fell in step beside him as they crossed her leaf-strewn yard. "I'm so sorry. How badly did he hurt you?"

Gage shrugged. "He only got in a lick or two, 'cause he caught me by surprise. But I think I set him straight." He grinned as he opened the passenger-side door for her. "I told him you were the sister I had my eye on."

She didn't look any less worried as she climbed into the truck cab. "Janet said he was in a bad mood the last couple of days. She's been tiptoeing around him and…" She blew out a gust of breath. "What a mess."

Gage said nothing else until he'd slid behind the steering wheel and pulled away from the curb. "But Janet's still covering for you at the diner tonight, right?"

Kate shook her head. "No, Laurie is. Janet didn't want to upset Larry. He's already so suspicious, and if Janet worked late…"

Gage squeezed the steering wheel tighter and bit back the remark that sprang to mind. He'd confront Kate soon enough with the purpose of this evening out. He steered the conversation to lighter topics for the short drive from Maple Cove to Honey Creek and the barbecue restaurant Hank Kelley's brother owned and operated.

For a Thursday night, Kelley's Cookhouse was bustling with customers, and the tangy scent of barbecue spiced the air. Gage kept an arm around Kate's shoulders as the hostess showed them to a table, then held her chair for her as they sat down. For his efforts, he earned one of Kate's sunny smiles.

"You're a dying breed, Gage."

"And what breed is that?" he asked as he took the chair kitty-corner to hers.

"You're a gentleman. Most men I know have basic manners, but not too many still hold doors or pull out chairs for ladies. I like that about you. Among other things." She grinned again and picked up her menu.

"My pleasure." He wanted to ask her what else she liked about him—what could she see in a gruff, washed-up soldier like him—but he bit back the question.

"So…are you a rib man?" Kate peered over the top of her menu. "The ribs here are really great."

"Maybe. I was thinking steak." Gage stared at his menu without really seeing it. How did he broach the topic he needed to discuss with Kate? She was so loyal to Janet that she was blind to her sister's manipulation. And as long as Janet had Kate to run to when things got tough, she had less motivation to leave her bad marriage.

He could put it off until after they'd eaten, but he'd never been one to delay the inevitable or shy away from difficult tasks.

"Mm…but the barbecued chicken sounds good, too." Kate licked her bottom lip and wiggled her eyebrows. "Maybe I'll get both."

"Kate." Gage put a hand on her arm to get her attention. "Can we talk about something…important?"

Her expression grew serious, and she lowered her menu. "What's wrong?"

"Good evening, folks. Welcome to Kelley's Cookhouse. Is this your first time here?"

Gage looked up to find an older, potbellied gentleman with short white hair and a cigar clamped in his mouth. Despite the amiable greeting, the man seemed grumpy, perhaps because the way he held the cigar clenched in his teeth made him look as though he was snarling. Gage didn't have to ask to know this was Donald Kelley, the owner of the restaurant and Hank's half-brother. The man had the same blue eyes as Cole and Hank.

Gage stood and extended a hand to Donald. "Good evening, Mr. Kelley. I'm Gage Prescott and—"

"I'm sorry," Donald said, pumping Gage's hand and slanting him a curious look. "Have we met?"

"No, sir. But your nephew, Cole, speaks highly of you and your restaurants, so we thought we'd give your food a try."

Donald's face brightened. "Any friend of Cole's is a friend of mine."

Gage cleared his throat, compelled to set the record straight. "Well, technically I'm just an acquaintance of Cole's. I'm staying at his ranch while I guard his father, Senator Henry Kelley."

The warmth faded from Donald's face. "You work for Hank?"

"Dylan hired me and my colleague to protect the senator in light of recent…threats."

Donald rolled his eyes. "You mean the bimbos he cheated with are making demands?"

Gage thought about the calls Hank had received from Gloria Cosgrove, but said only, "I'm not at liberty to say."

Donald grunted. "Of course." Then sobering, he added, "Are my brother or his family in any real danger?"

Gage pressed his mouth in a grim line. "I think you should talk to him about that."

The older man raised his eyebrows and nodded his understanding of what was left unsaid. "I see."

Gage shot a glance to Kate who sat silently, watching the exchange with polite patience. Clearing his throat, Gage flashed Kate a grateful smile and directed Donald's attention to his dinner companion. "And this beautiful lady is Kate Rogers, the best pastry chef in the northwest."

Donald greeted Kate, shaking her hand and giving her a nod of welcome. "A pastry chef, eh? Do you work anywhere around here?"

Kate nodded. "Ira's Diner in Maple Cove."

Donald blinked surprise. "Ira's Diner? Wait…so you're *that* pastry chef? Good gracious, gal, I've heard nothing but raves about your baking. In fact…" He glanced about the crowded room until his gaze latched on his target, and he waved a hand. "Bonnie Gene! Come 'ere. I have someone you have to meet!"

An average-height woman with shoulder-length brown hair and a gracious smile bustled over. As she approached the table, she divided a warm look between Gage and Kate. "Hello, I'm Bonnie Gene Kelley, Donald's wife. Welcome to Kelley's Cookhouse." Without breaking eye contact with Kate, Bonnie Gene reached up to snatch the cigar from Donald's mouth and tossed it in the bin of dirty dishes a busboy carried past them.

Donald grumbled something under his breath while Gage and Kate introduced themselves, then he announced, "Kate is the pastry chef you were raving about at Ira's Diner over in Maple Cove."

Bonnie Gene's eyes widened, and she pulled out a chair to sit down with them. "Oh my stars! I had your chocolate eclair when I was over visiting our nephew this summer. Perfection, my dear. Simply perfection."

"Thank you," Kate returned, blushing.

"And I bought several cinnamon buns to bring home for our breakfast the next morning, and even a day old, they were simply divine! How do you do it? Where did you learn to cook like that?" Bonnie Gene leaned closer as if expecting to learn a juicy secret.

A blush rose in Kate's cheeks. "I had a friend, a neighbor, who taught me to cook growing up."

"You mean you're not formally trained?" Bonnie Gene glanced at her husband. "Did you hear that, Donald?"

"I'm standing right here, aren't I?" Donald said under his breath.

Ignoring her husband's glib reply, Bonnie Gene caught Kate's hand in hers as if they were old, dear friends and huddled closer. "Who was this neighbor? Does she live around here? You really have the most amazing talent!"

Donald pulled out a chair and nodded toward it. "Mind if I sit?"

Gage really preferred that the couple not stay and chitchat. He'd brought Kate to Honey Creek in order to give them privacy for their conversation, away from the eyes of her friends and family in Maple Cove. Yet her reputation had followed them, as had Hank's. He gave a grudging nod to the chair. "Go ahead."

Donald sent him a dark look. "I'd like to know why my nephew thought his father needed a bodyguard. If there was a real problem, why didn't he contact the secret service? Can't they offer a senator protection?"

"I think Dylan wanted something more…personalized. More private."

Bonnie Gene turned to her husband, her face filled with animation and excitement. "Donald, give me your wallet. I want to show Kate a picture of our sweet Patience."

Donald dug in his back pants pocket. "Do Sarah or any of the kids have bodyguards?" he asked Gage.

Gage sighed. "Again, if you have questions, you should talk to Senator Kelley about it. I'm not free to discuss the matter."

"Senator Kelley?" Bonnie Gene piped in, hearing the snatch of his conversation with Donald. "You know Hank?"

"He's Hank's bodyguard," Donald said, handing his wife the wallet.

Bonnie Gene's mouth formed an O. Furrowing her brow in

concern, she leaned toward Gage. "What's happened? Why does Hank need a bodyguard?"

Gage opened his mouth to give his pat non-reply, when Donald said, "He won't say. He wants me to call Hank for answers."

"Well, I agree. You're brothers, for Pete's sake! If there's trouble enough that he needs a bodyguard...well, I think the time has come to make up with Hank. This squabble between you has gone on long enough."

"He's known where to find me for years if he wanted to patch things up." Donald glanced away, his jaw set.

Bonnie Gene punched his shoulder lightly. "So you be the bigger person and call him! You're just being stubborn. With the kids grown and marrying off, babies being born—" She waved the wallet she had yet to open. "—there's no time like the present to put an end to the feud that's kept you apart. This is a time for family. Have you ever thought that Hank could use a big brother right now?"

"What he needs is a good lawyer, if the news reports are any indication." Donald folded his arms over his chest.

Gage sat back and watched the exchange with open curiosity. He'd seen the overtures Hank had made toward Cole, clearly trying to repair the damage he'd done to that relationship. He'd also asked Cole about Donald. Maybe there was more hope of reconciling the two brothers than Donald thought.

"He's made mistakes, sure," Bonnie Gene said. "But haven't we all? I think you should stand behind him, give him some support and guidance."

"I think he might be open to a call from you." Gage surprised himself with his comment. His client's family business was not his concern. He needed to stay focused on his job, not get personally involved in a family drama.

But Bonnie Gene latched onto Gage's remark and smiled.

"See? I told you!" Then to Gage, "What did he say about Donald? Did he send you here to ask for a reconciliation?"

Gage raised a hand. "Nothing like that. I'm not even sure he knows I'm here. Cole recommended we come here...for our date." He added the last hoping Bonnie Gene would take a hint.

Donald did. He pushed back the chair he'd just taken and tugged his wife's arm. "Honey, let's let these two get back to their dinner."

The older woman wiggled free of her husband's grip. "In a minute. I haven't shown Kate our sweet baby yet." Bonnie Gene opened her husband's wallet, and an accordion-folded photo holder flopped out. "This," she said grandly, her smile beaming, "is our first grandbaby, Patience. Isn't she the most beautiful baby you've ever seen?"

Gage leaned closer to Kate for a peek at the pictures and glimpsed a red-haired cherub with blue eyes and slobbery grin. The kid was cute enough as babies went, he supposed. When he glanced up at Kate, the expression on his date's face stole his breath.

Kate stared at the baby pictures with a teary, lovestruck gaze. The longing that filled her expression tore at Gage's heart, and a sinking reality settled over him as cold and heavy as stone. He'd known he was a bad fit for Kate all along, but seeing the hope and bittersweet emotion that flooded Kate's face when she gazed at the baby pictures brought the harsh truth into focus. What Kate needed, dreamed of and deserved were things that left him in a cold sweat. Marriage, children, a home brimming with love and laughter.

How could he offer her stability and family when his life was a nightmarish mess? The darkness that clouded his life would eventually eclipse her light and smother the sweetness that made her the woman he'd come to love.

"Oh," Kate said on a sigh. "She is precious. You have every

reason to be proud." She pulled her bottom lip between her teeth, and Gage would swear she was fighting not to cry.

Gage glanced at Donald, who wore an expression similar to his wife's. For all his stubborn refusal to reconnect with his half-brother, Donald Kelley was clearly a proud grandpa.

"Kate, honey," Bonnie Gene said, again clasping his date's hand as if they were long-lost family, "what would I have to do to steal you away from Ira's Diner?"

Kate raised a startled expression from the baby pictures. "Steal me?"

"For our restaurants." Bonnie Gene sent her husband a look that asked, "Isn't this a good idea?" Donald raised his eyebrows and nodded subtly. "You could either work here or at one of the others in the chain. Although I'll admit," Bonnie Gene added, "I'd love to have you here rather than another location so I'll benefit from your delicious baking!"

Kate smiled politely. "Thank you, but I'm not looking to change jobs. I'm really quite happy where I am."

"We'll match whatever salary you're making at Ira's and add ten thousand to it. Plus benefits," Donald said.

Kate goggled at the couple. "That's...very generous, but I...I don't..."

"Please think about it at least, Kate." Bonnie Gene squeezed Kate's hand and gave her a beseeching smile. "You're the best pastry chef in the area, hands down, and we want the best for our restaurants. We could even let you develop your own special dessert menu with your private recipes."

"A tempting offer, to be sure." Kate took one last longing look at the baby photos before handing them to Bonnie Gene with a trembling hand. "I—I'll think about it."

Gage eyed his date with concern. She looked completely overwhelmed...because of the employment offer or because of the baby pictures?

As Bonnie Gene and Donald excused themselves and

moved on to greet other diners, Gage gave Kate a moment to gather her composure. Knowing how emotional Kate still was, he hated to raise the topic that needed to be broached. Rusty's warning echoed in his head, and Gage acknowledged that by confronting Kate about her family issues, he could be ruining any chance of a future with her. But then, in the past several days, the wide gulf of differences between them had become abundantly clear.

He choked back the swell of despondency that swamped him when he acknowledged how wrong he was for Kate. Building a relationship with Kate had been a pipe dream. He'd been drawn to her because she exuded all the qualities his life needed, and he'd greedily sucked in her goodness and joy like a dry sponge. But soon he would become a drain on her, much the way Janet was now.

"Wow. A job offer. That was…unexpected." Kate lifted a shaky smile.

"Shouldn't be unexpected. You're a great cook, and thanks to your work at the diner, people know it. I wouldn't be surprised if this weren't the first of many offers."

She dismissed the idea with a wave of her hand and stuck her nose in the menu again.

"It's a great opportunity. You should take it."

"Can't," she said from behind the menu.

He pulled the menu down to meet her gaze. "Why not?"

Her shoulders drooped. "Because…I came to Montana for Janet. I took the job at Ira's so I could be near her, keep an eye on her, help her out. That hasn't changed."

Which brought them to the topic he needed to discuss with her. He took a deep breath, knowing she wouldn't like what he had to say. "Maybe it's time it did change. Maybe Janet won't leave Larry because you're coddling her."

Her eyebrows snapped together. "What?"

A waitress stepped up to their table to take their orders,

so he stifled his answer for the time being. But as soon as they'd each ordered, he tackled the subject again.

"With you, Janet has a safety net in place, someone to pick up her slack and make it easy for her to ignore the truth. You're like the enabler who keeps coming to the rescue for the alcoholic. As long as she can manipulate you and use you, she has less incentive to stand on her own two feet."

Kate lifted her chin, and the usual sparkle in her eyes became a gleam of anger. "Janet is nothing like an alcoholic. Her situation is completely different. And...how exactly do you think I'm enabling her?"

"Giving her a place to run when Larry gets violent. Working extra shifts so she can cater to her husband's jealousy and unreasonable demands." Kate started shaking her head, but Gage persisted. "Giving up close friends and a life you loved to move across the country to 'look out' for her. Passing up golden opportunities to further your career so you can take care of her."

She huffed impatiently. "I'm supposed to turn away my own sister, my only family, when she comes to me saying her husband has hit her?"

"Look at it this way. If she had nowhere to go to escape when things got ugly, if she had to stay and face the painful truth of her marriage each time Larry got violent, how long would she put up with him then? Maybe you have to let her hit rock bottom and stop giving her a temporary escape hatch before she'll face the truth."

"Tough love? That's your idea of how to help an abused wife? She's not some teenager who's acting out. Her husband's abuse is not her fault!"

"But her *response* to it is her choice. You're making it easier for her to live in denial."

Kate sighed in disgust and jerked the menu up again.

"At the very least, you're letting your sister dictate your

life. She knows you'll do anything for her, even if it inconveniences you, and she uses that to her full advantage. Maybe because she feels she has no control over her own life, so she manipulates your life, where she does have the control."

"Janet doesn't manipulate or control me."

"Really? Prove it. Take the Kelleys' job offer."

"I told you I can't. I—" She stopped abruptly, her expression shocked, as if she finally heard herself, finally realized what she was doing. Tears puddled in her eyes.

Gage reached for her hand and pitched his voice low. "Kate, I saw your face when you were looking at those baby pictures. That's what you want for yourself, isn't it? A husband, babies, a family like the Zooks?"

She didn't answer right away. Instead she held his gaze, tears slipping free of her eyelashes and trickling down her cheeks. Each tear was a sucker punch to his gut, because they confirmed what he'd known all along. Kate wanted things he couldn't give her. How could a tormented ex-soldier, who'd seen and done things that still gave him nightmares, ever give a woman with a pure heart like Kate's any kind of stability or happiness?

"What's wrong with wanting those things?" she asked in a hoarse whisper.

"Nothing. You deserve that life, Kate. But how can you find that happiness while you're tied to Janet?"

"So I'm supposed to turn my back on my abused sister so I can be happy?" She shook her head. "I'm sorry, but I'm not that selfish."

"Janet is. Has she once put your needs in front of her own? Or does she demand more and more of your time and energy to help her with Larry? She wouldn't even cover for you tonight, so you could have a well-deserved night out."

Kate gripped the edge of the table and leaned toward him, her expression defensive and angry. "Why do you care anyway? What business is it of yours what I do or how I deal with my family's problems? What makes you think you can waltz into town and tell me how to live my life when you've only known me for two weeks?"

He released a slow breath of frustration. "I know what I'm saying sounds harsh, but I don't believe in whitewashing the truth."

"Did I ask for your opinion? Your job is to protect Senator Kelley, not micro-manage my life."

Gage tensed. She was right, of course. He'd sworn not to get involved, needed to stay focused on the job he'd been hired to do. So why was he interfering?

One look in her sky-blue eyes, now flashing angrily at him, and he knew why. "I only said what I did because..." He paused and swallowed hard, facing a difficult truth himself. "I've grown to care about you, Kate. More than I should care, since I have nothing to offer you except heartache. But the fact is...I'm falling in love with you."

Gage's confession took the steam out of Kate. She rocked back in her chair and stared at him with her heart in her throat. She'd felt the connection, the chemistry between them growing every time they were together but...*love?* Did she love him? Could she love him?

In the last two weeks, she'd told him a great deal about herself, her history, her dreams, her issues with Janet. But what did she really know about him? He seemed to shut down when she questioned him about his life. What answers she did get were terse and generic. She sensed a gentle and caring soul buried beneath his gruff, tough-guy exterior. Why else would he be so concerned about her relationship with Janet—even if she didn't like his take on the matter?

And what about his earlier comment that he had nothing

to offer her but heartache? What did he know that he'd not told her?

Their food arrived, buying her a little time to formulate a response to his bombshell. *I'm falling in love with you.* If he was falling for her, what did he plan to do about it? He was only in town temporarily on assignment. What kind of future did he have in mind for them?

While her head buzzed with questions, a plate of ribs she no longer had an appetite for was slid in front of her. The tangy scent of her dinner teased her nose, but she pushed the plate away. More than food, right now she needed answers.

Gage had yet to tuck into his steak, and as he met her gaze, his words still hung between them. His eyes darkened and burrowed into her. "Can we forget I said that?"

"Not if you meant it." She unfolded her napkin and slipped it on her lap, merely to busy her trembling hands. "Gage, I have feelings for you, too. I'd think that was obvious, but...I really don't know what to do with those feelings."

"That makes two of us," he said quietly. He picked up his knife and fork and cut his steak. "The last thing I want to do is hurt you."

She plucked a French fry from her plate then dropped it again when it burnt her fingers. "What makes you think you'd hurt me?"

He sighed but wouldn't look at her. "Because I'm totally unprepared for the kind of relationship you deserve. My life is not in a place where I can..." Rather than finish his sentence, he scowled down at his plate. When he finally met her gaze, his eyes were stormy. "I'm still dealing with a lot of baggage from my last tour in Afghanistan."

She knitted her brow in concern and reached for his hand. "What kind of things? What happened to you over there, Gage?"

He didn't answer, nor did he pull his hand away. A muscle

in his jaw twitched as he clenched his teeth. Tension radiated from him like waves of heat off of pavement.

She recalled his reaction to the backfiring truck the week before. He'd been thoroughly shaken, revisiting some trauma, the memories making him tremble and sweat.

What kind of nightmare had he lived through?

"Tell me about it, Gage. Please."

His eyes snapped up to meet hers again. Taking a deep breath as if rousing himself from deep thoughts, he slipped his hand out from under hers. "It's hardly appropriate dinner conversation."

Disappointment and a stab of rejection wrenched inside her. "You know my greatest hopes, my deepest pain, my biggest fears and troubles. You can even sit there and dish out your opinion on how I should handle my life, but your life is taboo? A bit hypocritical, don't you think, Gage?"

"Kate…"

"Why can't you trust me with what's bothering you?"

He jabbed a bite of meat in his mouth and chewed for a moment. "It's not that I don't trust you. I just don't want to burden you with the nightmares I live with. Your life, with the exception of Janet's problems with Larry, is about sweetness and joy and the simple pleasures. I love that about you. You're a breath of fresh air to me, and I won't let the sewage of my past ruin that."

Kate shuffled her French fries around on her plate, her heart heavy. "If you can't open up to me, can't talk to me about what happened, how are we supposed to build a relationship?"

"We aren't. That's what I'm saying. I can't start something with you that I know will hurt you down the road."

She frowned at him. "I'm a big girl, Gage. Why don't you let me be the judge of what I can and can't handle emotionally?"

"Maybe I'm the one who can't handle what a relationship would mean. Maybe I'm still too raw to feel anything real and meaningful."

Sympathy battered her heart. She heard such grief in his voice. "Then let my love heal you. We can work through whatever happened to you together, if you'd let me help." When he didn't respond, she added, "You said you were falling in love with me. How—"

"I shouldn't have said that."

An ache sliced through her. Why was he shutting her out? She had to find a way past his defenses. Beneath his pain, Gage was a good man, a loving man, a gentle man. The kind of man she wanted to plan a future with.

"I'm falling in love with you, too, Gage."

He set his fork down, leveled a piercing gaze on her and whispered, "Don't."

She frowned. "Don't what? Care about you? Help you? Be there for you?"

"All of the above," he said flatly, his expression dark and troubled.

She laughed without humor and waved a hand around the table. "If you don't want a relationship with me, what is all this about? Why did you ask me out?"

His shoulders stiffened. "Because... I needed to talk to you where we wouldn't be distracted."

He looked as if he was going to say more, but when he clamped his mouth shut and glanced away, she finished for him. "About Janet."

"Yeah."

Pain slashed through her chest. The hope that she'd harbored earlier in the evening that she was on the verge of a meaningful and treasured relationship with Gage burst in to a thousand prickling shards.

She tossed her napkin on the table and took her purse from

the back of her chair. "And we have talked about your views on Janet's situation, so I guess dinner is over."

He scowled at her. "Kate, no...you haven't even eaten."

"Suddenly I'm not hungry."

He set his fork down, and his expression paled. "Kate, I'm sorry. I never wanted to mislead you, but—"

"But you did. Those kisses we shared weren't chaste tokens of friendship." Her exasperation and hurt bubbled up, filling her voice with the tremble of emotion. "I felt something special happening between us. When you held me the other day, I felt something deep and powerful. An electricity and passion and intimate connection that goes beyond casual friendship. I know you felt it, too. After the way you kissed me, what was I supposed to think when you asked me out?"

"Exactly what you *did* think. I felt the connection, too. I can't stop thinking about you, Kate, even when I'm supposed to be working. I've never met a woman who has meant more to me than you do."

"Then why are you afraid to take a chance on us?"

"It's not fear, Kate. I'm trying to protect you." He paused, swallowing hard, and the haunted expression he wore shook her to the core. "If I don't walk away from you now, eventually the demons of my past would destroy everything I love about you. And I'd never forgive myself if I let that happen."

Chapter 12

The drive back to Maple Cove was somber and quiet. Gage tuned Rusty's radio, which only picked up AM stations, to a call-in show where the host was leading a discussion on voters' disenchantment with their elected leaders. Senator Henry Kelley's recent fall from grace was covered in depth, including speculation about his retreat from the public eye.

Gage cast a worried glance across the front seat to Kate, wanting desperately to do or say something to mitigate the misery he'd caused. She stared out at the night-shrouded scenery, her face lined with dejection and disappointment.

When he pulled up in front of her house, she sent him a tight, emotionless smile. "Thank you for dinner. Good luck with—"

When he reached for her, sliding his hand along her jaw to cup her cheek, she caught her breath and closed her eyes.

"Forgive me, Kate. I know I've hurt you, but…it's better this way. I'm all wrong for you. You deserve a life I don't know how to give you."

She pulled her chin from his grip and opened the truck door. "At least be honest about what this is. You know what I want from you, but you're too scared to try. I just wish I understood the real reason why."

Without giving him a chance to respond, she slid off the seat and closed the door behind her. He watched until she disappeared inside the yellow warmth of her house, then drove back to the ranch with a knot in his gut.

Too scared to try. Every time her voice echoed in his mind, he mentally flinched away from it. Could it be there was some painful truth to her assessment?

He parked Rusty's truck by the bunkhouse and, when he stepped out of the cab, the vast Montana sky and lonely moon called to him. Before retiring for the night, Gage wandered down past the holding pens and climbed up into the hayloft of the barn. From there, he meandered over to the loft door, sat down in the opening and propped himself against the wooden door frame to look out at the star-filled night and think. He'd hurt Kate with his decree, he knew, but he still believed it was better that he break things off now, before they grew any closer, than risk hurting her even worse in the long run.

Let my love heal you. We can work through whatever happened to you together, if you let me help.

But he didn't want to be another drain on Kate's life. She already had too much stress and strife with her sister. He didn't want to burden her with his troubled past. His past was something he had to work through on his own. Her optimism and willingness to tie herself to him, despite his baggage, burrowed deep to his soul. He'd never had anyone as generous and caring in his life before, and Kate's love was a treasured gift he'd cherish.

He let the sounds of the night—the nickering of horses, the chirp of crickets and the gentle stir of breeze—flow through him, but he doubted anything would ease the ache in his heart that losing Kate caused. He closed his eyes to picture her sweet smile, knowing he'd made the best decision he could—for her.

As the autumn chill seeped into him, a noise he identified first as a cow in distress filtered through the night's calm. He opened his eyes and strained to peer through the darkness into the night. Had a wild animal attacked the herd?

When the noise came again, he recognized it as a human voice, a man's voice. A cry for help.

Alarm streaked through Gage, and he jumped to his feet, using the elevation of the barn loft to his advantage to scan the ranch yard and pastures. The night beyond the lights of the barn and stable shrouded the fields in inky blackness, but the voice came again, low and pained. "Help me!"

Gage hurried down from the barn loft and ran into the ranch yard, drawing his weapon as he scanned the property. "Who's there?"

"It's me. Rusty…"

At the edge of the circle of light from the barn, Gage saw a dark shadow that transformed into a horse and rider. The man atop the horse was slumped in the saddle, riding draped along the horse's neck with one leg dangling awkwardly at his side.

"Please, I need…a doctor. Hurt…" Rusty gasped, his voice thick with pain.

"Rusty, what happened?" Gage rushed forward, reholstering his gun to free his hands. He grabbed Red's reins, stopping the animal.

The ranch manager raised his head only far enough to meet Gage's eyes. The man's face was battered and swollen. Blood had dried at his nose and lip. "Think my…leg is broken."

Gage's pulse spiked as he saw the odd angle of Rusty's leg and his obvious facial injuries. "Good God, what happened to you?"

Rusty shook his head. "Just…help me get…to my house."

Gage snatched out his cell phone and dialed Cole's number. "Call an ambulance, then meet me down near the barn. It's Rusty Moore. He's hurt pretty bad." Without waiting for a reply, he disconnected and stowed his phone. Then reaching up to brace Rusty under his arms, he caught the older man as he slid off his horse.

Rusty screamed in pain as the movement jostled his broken leg, and the anguish in the man's cry ricocheted through Gage's memory.

Soldiers with twisted limbs or bullet holes in their gut crying out for rescue from a battlefield. Gage's breath hung in his lungs, and he fought down the surge of bile in his throat.

Focus. Do your job.

He absorbed Rusty's weight, careful not to bump the man's injured leg, and eased him to the ground. The angle of Rusty's leg told Gage the break was bad. Really bad. At his thigh. And clearly excruciating.

Gage's stomach churned.

He dredged his memory for the battlefield first aid he'd been taught. Triage.

Gage gently probed Rusty's ribs and arms, searching out other injuries. Though the leg and facial injuries seemed to be the worst of his wounds, his whole body had been battered and bruised. The man needed attention soon. By the look of it, pain was already sending Rusty into shock. Gage yanked off his jacket and laid it over Rusty's chest to ward of the evening chill.

When he tried to examine the injured leg, Rusty groaned in agony, his head rocking side to side.

The sound of running steps preceded Cole's arrival. "Rusty!" Cole skidded to a stop, dropping to his knees beside his ranch manager. "Hang on, partner. An ambulance is on its way." He glanced up at Gage. "What can I do?"

"I don't know that there is much we can do until the ambulance gets here. His femur is broken, and that's gotta hurt like hell. I think he's shocky."

Cole nodded. "What the hell happened?"

Gage shrugged. "Don't know. He just came riding up, slumped over and calling for help."

Cole leaned over Rusty. "Hold on, friend. Help's coming." He drew a deep shuddering breath and blew it out. "What happened to you? How did you get hurt?"

Rusty closed his eyes and moaned. "Red…got spooked. Threw me. My foot…caught in the…stirrup." He paused. Swallowed hard, grimacing, clearly in horrible pain. "Red… dragged me."

Dragged? Gage winced internally. That had to hurt. Your whole body being bumped and battered across the rocks and dirt…

Gage bit the inside of his cheek, mulling over Rusty's story. The ranch manager was an experienced horseman. Even if Red had spooked, Rusty shouldn't have been thrown. Twenty minutes later, after the ambulance had pulled out of the ranch drive, carrying Rusty to the hospital in Honey Creek, Gage pulled Cole aside.

"Does it seem odd to you that a rider of Rusty's skill would be thrown from his horse, would allow his foot to become tangled in the stirrup so that he's dragged?"

Cole frowned. "Are you calling Rusty a liar?"

Gage shrugged, not taking the edge of hostility in Cole's voice personally. He was, after all, challenging the honesty of one of Cole's valued ranch employees, and, as Hank's bodyguard, his presence at the ranch had to feel like an inconvenience to Cole. "Just seems odd to me. It doesn't quite add up."

Glancing away with a heavy sigh, Cole shook his head.

"Rusty has worked for me for years. I trust him implicitly. I can't imagine him lying without good reason."

"And what qualifies as a good reason to lie to your boss?" Gage pushed.

Cole sent him a sharp look, then dragged a hand over his mouth. "All the more reason to believe him. Rusty doesn't lie."

"In light of the attack on your father's car and the breaches of the ranch security while you were gone, I think you should be especially vigilant in the coming weeks. All indications are that your dad's enemies know he's staying here, and they could try to get at him through you, through your ranch."

Cole held his gaze for several long seconds, his expression grave as he considered Gage's warning. "What exactly is going on with my dad? This can't all be related to the affairs he had. Something bigger is at work, isn't it?"

Gage gave the rancher an apologetic look. "I'm not at liberty to say. You'll have to talk to him yourself."

Cole gave a terse nod. Sighed. "Well…thanks. For your help tonight with Rusty. And…for everything you're doing for my father."

Gage heard the unspoken affection for his father behind Cole's thanks. For the family's sake, he hoped Hank could bridge the distance with his children. If any good could come out of the ugly predicament Hank had gotten himself in with the nefarious secret society, perhaps it would be a renewed relationship with his son.

Gage woke the next morning to the sound of raised voices. A frisson of alarm streaked through him as he threw on his jeans. Following the sound of the voices, he hurried down the hall, concerned that some new attack had been made on the ranch or that Bart might need backup protecting Hank.

When he entered the kitchen, he found Cole and Hank

squared off, shouting at each other. Bart hung back, cradling a mug of coffee, letting the father and son vent.

"I can't believe you let me leave last week without saying anything!" Cole shouted, his cheeks red with fury.

"I tried to tell you, but you stormed out and—"

"She's my sister! I deserved to know!"

Apparently Hank had finally come clean with Cole about Lana's kidnapping. Gage shifted his weight, uncomfortable with the open hostility.

"Maybe I was trying to spare you the worry, considering everything else that's going on with roundup—"

Cole scoffed hotly. "Don't give me that! You don't think about anyone but yourself. You didn't say anything because somehow you thought not telling me was in *your* best interest."

Gage stepped backward, trying to ease out of the kitchen unnoticed. The family argument wasn't his business, and he had thirty minutes to shower and dress before his shift officially began.

"Prescott—" Cole's address stopped him mid-escape. "Did you know about this, too?"

Gage gave Cole a level look. "I did."

"Yet you said nothing. Even last night when Rusty was hurt."

Gage raised his chin. "How is Rusty?"

Cole shook his head. "Holding his own at the hospital in Honey Creek." He shifted his glare to Hank. "And what's been done to find Lana? To rescue her?"

"I've handled it," Senator Kelley said, tugging on the sleeves of his bathrobe as if he were straightening a tailored suit for a high-powered meeting.

Cole narrowed a skeptical glare on his father. "How?"

As Hank launched into an explanation of the mercenary he'd sent after Lana and Cole argued to bring in the FBI,

Gage slipped back to his room for a hot shower and a bottle of aspirin for the raging headache already throbbing at his temples.

He hadn't slept well. Thoughts of Kate and their disastrous evening had taunted him all night, along with visions of Rusty's maimed leg and cries of anguish. When he had dosed off, his sleep had been peppered with dreams of roadside bombs and dead soldiers pointing accusing fingers at him. His bleak mood this morning only confirmed that he'd made the right choice telling Kate goodbye last night. He couldn't in good conscience subject her to the dark torment he dealt with on a daily basis.

He would desperately miss the light and hope she had given him, even if only for these last few days.

When his shift started, he made his way back to the kitchen where Hank still nursed a cup of coffee as he sat staring bleakly out the window watching the activity at the stockyard, and presumably, Cole's part in the ranch work.

"Don't start," Hank groused without looking away from the window.

"Sir?" Gage pulled up a chair and joined Hank at the table.

"With the I-told-you-sos. I should have told Cole about Lana sooner. I should have called in the FBI. I should have reported the Raven's Head Society to the authorities." He sighed wearily and cut a desolate look to Gage. "I'm doing the best I can. I'm trying to deal with a bad situation without making it worse."

Gage rubbed his freshly shaven jaw and met Hank's gaze. "Perhaps it's time to change strategies."

The senator stared at him dispiritedly before returning his attention to the activity out the window. Gage took the opportunity to pour himself a cup of coffee and rip a banana from the bunch on the counter. As he settled at the table again, the senator's new secure cell phone chirped.

Hank pulled out the phone and checked the screen. Scowled. Then blanched.

He jerked his gaze up to Gage's, his eyes wide. "It's a text message from Garrison, the man I sent to find Lana."

Gage's pulse tripped, and his muscles tensed, bracing for bad news. "And?"

"He's finally in place, ready to move, but he wants his money before he goes in."

Gage furrowed his brow. "How did he get the number for your secured line?"

Hank shrugged. "I don't know. My assistant Cindy must have given it to him. I told her to find him, to find out what was taking so long... I—" Hank looked at the cell when it chirped again, announcing a new message. "He wants it sent to an offshore account in the Caymans. This morning, by eleven. Says to see a man named George Lucas at the First Montana Land Bank in town. He's given me an account number and—"

"May I?" Gage reached for the phone and read the text messages for himself. "You're sure this is from Garrison?"

Hank nodded. "The number the message was sent from is the phone I gave him to call me with." The senator released a deep breath, and a smile ghosted across his lips. "Finally. Maybe by tonight, Lana will be here, and with her out of danger, I can turn in the people behind this nightmare and get my life back."

Gage handed the phone back to Hank. "What are you going to do?"

Squaring his shoulders, Hank flattened his hands on the tabletop and pushed to his feet. "I'm going to the bank to transfer money to Garrison's account. Get the car."

Kate went through the motions—baking, serving and cleaning up breakfast at the diner—but her mind was anywhere but on her work. After her heartbreaking dinner with Gage, she'd wanted nothing more than to crawl into bed and lick her wounds. But Janet had shown up on her doorstep, sporting another black eye and pleading for Kate to take her in "until Larry cooled off."

And something inside Kate had clicked. She wasn't convinced Gage's method of helping her abused sister was the right way, the loving way, the supportive way. But she knew she'd heard the same excuses, forgiven the same denials and catered to the same needs from her sister too many times.

And she'd turned Janet away.

"Go to one of the women's shelters I've told you about. They have professional counselors there and experts who can help you file a restraining order against Larry," she'd told her shocked sister.

"Kate, what are you doing? Let me in!" Janet had cried.

"You have to leave him, Janet. Because I'm through helping you live this lie." Tears had leaked onto her cheeks as she'd stood her ground. "When he's out of your life and you're ready to make a fresh start somewhere, I'll be there for you. But as long as you stay with him, I'm done."

And she'd closed and locked her door with Janet standing slack-jawed on her front porch.

In the hours since she'd turned her back on her sister, Kate had doubted herself, castigated herself and tried multiple times to reach Janet on her cell. Without luck.

Janet hadn't shown up at work hours later. But Larry had. He'd been contrite, looking for his wife and spewing the same meaningless reassurances that he'd change. Kate had told him, quite honestly, that she didn't know where Janet was, and he'd left in a huff.

An hour later, an unfamiliar number lit Kate's cell. She answered with a tentative, "Hello?"

"It's me. I ditched my old phone so Larry couldn't call me."

Kate wilted with relief at the sound of her sister's voice. "Thank God! I've been so worried about you! I'm sorry about last night. I—"

"Don't be. It was just the wake-up call I needed. You were right...about everything." Janet's voice cracked and with it, so did Kate's heart.

She clutched the phone tighter and struggled for a breath. "Where are you? How can I help?"

"Idaho. I'm at a shelter, but...I'd rather not say where. I'm getting help here and..." Janet paused. "...I don't think I'm coming back. Not as long as Larry is in Maple Cove."

Kate's knees gave out, and she sank into a chair by the table she'd been wiping clean. "I...don't know what to say. I'm proud of you, Janet. This...couldn't be easy for you. But it's the right thing. And I'll support you however I can—"

"You already have." Janet paused and sniffled. "Y-you've put your life on hold for me long enough. It's your turn to follow your heart and m-make your dreams come true. I know you want more than working in a little diner in Podunk, Montana."

Kate thought of the job offer the Kelleys had made just last night. Maybe...

"—with Gage," Janet was saying. Gage's name snapped Kate's attention back to her sister's tearful apology. "I know how much you like him. I think he's one of the good ones, Katie. Don't let him get away."

Kate's heart twisted, and she swallowed a painful knot in her throat. No point telling Janet that Gage had ended their relationship last night before it had really begun. She stared numbly at the coffee rings on the paper place mats, while she told Janet she loved her, would always support her and wished her luck with her new life. After Janet hung up, Kate sat quietly, staring into near space for several minutes, until

Laurie came out of the kitchen with a zipped money bag and found her. "The deposit is ready for you to take to the bank."

Kate blinked Laurie into focus and offered a half-hearted smile. "Thanks."

Because the Maple Cove branch of the First Montana Land Bank didn't have a secure location for businesses to make a deposit after hours, Kate always delivered the daily deposit for the diner when the bank opened each morning. She accepted the money bag from Laurie and shoved to her feet.

"Hey, you okay?" Laurie asked, frowning her concern.

Kate tried harder for a convincing smile. "Yeah, I'll be fine." *Even if my life has turned on its head in the last twelve hours.*

"Worried about Janet?" Laurie asked with a knowing tilt to her head.

Kate hesitated. "No. Not really." And with a freeing swell of assurance in her chest, she knew that was the truth. She told Laurie about Janet's call. "My sister is strong, capable, resilient. She's going to be fine."

Kate tucked the money bag under her arm and headed out of the diner. The bank was a short walk down the street, and she welcomed the chance to get out of the diner for a few minutes. Happy though she was for Janet's breakthrough, she hoped the bracing October wind, blowing in a new cold front, would help sweep away the lingering doubts and confusion about her own future. She was finally free to pursue the life she wanted...but the man she wanted at the center of that life had walked away from her just last night. The irony stabbed her with a searing pain.

She tightened her fist around the deposit bag and blinked away the sting of tears. She refused to play the poor-pitiful-me part in this scenario. Gage might not be willing to take a chance on her, but she wouldn't give up on him so easily. Not when he was so clearly hurting and shutting himself off from the world in a mistaken sense of self-preservation. If her sister could find the courage to make a bold, if frightening, change for the best, how could she shy away from a fight for the man with whom she'd fallen in love?

As he drove to Maple Cove, Gage eyed the dark sky to the north. The weatherman called today's cold and wind normal for October, but the black clouds reminded Gage of the front still days away that could cause trouble for Cole getting his herd to market. The gloomy weather also sent a chill deep into Gage's bones that warned him something ominous could be coming for him as well.

Or maybe he was just projecting his bad mood over his breakup with Kate onto anyone and anything he saw that morning. Bart had given him a wide berth before he and Hank left the ranch. And Hank, despite his hopefulness that his ordeal was drawing to a close, had commented on Gage's surliness. He'd blamed it on his lack of sleep and killer head-ache, rather than admit the real root of his unrest.

He'd only said goodbye to Kate last night and already he missed her. He missed the idea of knowing he could visit her at the diner or at her house and be buoyed simply by her pres-ence. But his mind was set, his choice made. Giving Kate up was what was best for her. Even if it was killing him.

Gage found a parking place near the bank and met Hank's gaze in the rearview mirror. "You sure you couldn't transfer the funds electronically or with a phone call? I don't like you being exposed this way."

"The directions were specific. I'm supposed to meet with the manager, Mr. Lucas, to make the transaction. I don't want to give Garrison any reason not to follow through on his end."

"Fine," Gage grumbled, "let's go then." He gritted his teeth and braced himself against the cold north wind as he fol-lowed Hank to the concrete steps of the First Montana Land

Bank. Gage held the door for Hank, then swept an encompassing gaze around the bank as he stepped inside. Inside, the small-town institution was much like the ones in larger towns. Marble floors, velvet ropes separating the lines for the tellers, loan officers ensconced in small offices on each side with large plate glass windows to the main lobby. A handful of customers waited in line to do their business with the tellers—an older woman he remembered seeing at Ira's Diner, a frazzled mother with two small, active children, and—

Kate. Gage's heart gave a kick.

Just as he spotted her, she turned, as if feeling his gaze, and the bored look she'd worn morphed into an expression of heartbreaking longing and regret. He tamped the urge that swelled in his chest to cross the lobby to her and fold her in his arms, promise her that whatever stood in their way could be resolved.

But how could he make such promises? Nothing had changed. He was who he was, and he refused to burden her with his past. Their paths might have crossed, but that didn't change the fact that they had very different lives and were headed in opposite directions.

"Excuse me." Hank's voice, as he stopped a woman with a bank name tag, pulled Gage back to the business at hand. "I was told to see a man named George Lucas. Can you tell me where his office is?"

The woman smiled. "Somewhere in Hollywood, I'd assume."

"Pardon?" Hank didn't look amused.

"The director? He did all the *Star Wars* movies." The woman's grin vanished when Hank glared at her. "I'm sorry, sir, but there's no one at this bank named—"

"Nobody move!" a man shouted.

Gage whirled toward the source of the shout, while reaching under his jacket for his gun.

Across the lobby, two men, one tall and barrel-chested, the other much shorter and thin, waved revolvers at the bank's patrons. Both wore ski masks to hide their faces. The lone security guard for the bank lay in a crumpled heap at the first man's feet. "Do what we say, and no one has to get hurt! Put your hands in the air and get on your knees. Everyone! Now!"

The bigger man glanced toward Gage, saw his weapon and aimed his gun at Gage's heart. "Don't try to be a hero, wiseguy."

Gage held firm, stepping smoothly in front of Hank. "Drop your weapon."

The big guy jerked his head toward the smaller man, then nodded toward Kate, who knelt closest to them. The second thug grabbed Kate by the hair and dragged her to her feet. Kate gasped in pain and fear.

An icy chill raced through Gage. Not Kate! Please, no!

"Do something!" Hank grated in a hushed voice behind him. "Shoot them!"

But he couldn't fire on the men without putting Kate at risk. The smaller man held his weapon to Kate's temple, his thin arm around her throat as he towed her backward. Kate stumbled and struggled, her panicked gaze glued on Gage's. Her eyes pleaded with him for help while she gasped for air through the thug's viselike hold across her neck.

"You drop your gun, or the lady takes a bullet," the first man said, glowering at Gage.

What to do? Lower his weapon and put his client at risk or hold his position and put Kate in danger? Gage gritted his teeth, hating the odds against him. Two against one. They had a hostage. He had to play the odds if he had a prayer of keeping not only Kate and Hank safe, but the other bank customers and employees. If bullets started flying...

His gut churning with a horrid sense of failure, he raised one palm and set his revolver on the floor.

"Good." The first thug smirked through the mouth opening of his ski mask. "Now kick it over to me."

Gage gave the revolver a small push with his toe, but not nearly the kick needed for his gun to reach the thug.

The big guy's eyes narrowed, and, as he moved toward Gage's weapon he yelled to the room, "Everyone toss your wallets on the floor and kick them to me. No tricks or you can be the first to die."

Around him the patrons and employees scurried to comply. Gage added his wallet to the growing pile, feeling a sense of impotent rage building in him.

"You too, pops." The man waved his gun toward Hank as he collected both Gage's gun and wallet from the floor.

Gage glanced at his client, who glared stubbornly at the thief. "Do it, sir. Don't get shot over the cash in your wallet and a couple of credit cards."

The senator cast Gage a look of disgust that said, *Some protection you are,* then tossed his wallet to the robber.

Where were the police? Surely one of the bank tellers had managed to trigger a silent alarm by now. What was taking the small town's police so long to arrive?

The big guy gathered the wallets into a paper sack then backed toward a side stairwell door—no doubt the way they'd come in without being detected until it was too late.

The smaller man tugged Kate with him as he backed toward the door, his revolver still hovering at Kate's head. Gage's heart thundered against his ribs. Why hadn't they let Kate go?

Suddenly the bigger man turned and ran out the door. The smaller man followed, dragging Kate with him into the stairwell, and the door slammed shut with a hollow bang. While the stunned patrons glanced nervously from one to another and struggled to their feet, Gage ran to the fallen security guard, drew the guard's weapon and shouted to Hank, "Get in an office and lock the door. Stay there until I get back!"

Haunted by the terror that had filled Kate's eyes, Gage ran toward the stairwell door in pursuit of the bank robbers. An uneasy feeling chased down his spine as he crashed through the heavy door. Too many things about the holdup didn't make sense, but he didn't pause to work through the oddities.

The men had Kate. Nothing else was important until he knew she was safe.

Chapter 13

"Hurry up!" Kate's captor muttered as she was shoved down the sidewalk at gunpoint. "I don't want to hurt you, but if you give us any trouble, I will kill you! So help me God, I will. We've come too far in this to let you blow it for us now!"

Kate frowned, startled. The voice belonged to a woman, not a man as she'd assumed. When she jerked her head around to stare more closely at her kidnapper, she met the woman's icy stare. Long, mascara-caked eyelashes and umber eyeshadow framed the pale blue eyes that stared back at her through the ski mask.

"Who are you? What do you want from me?" Kate asked, stumbling to keep up as the woman dragged her along the sidewalk.

The woman's accomplice had peeled off in the opposite direction and disappeared down an alley beside the bank just as Kate and the woman had emerged from the bank into the cool October morning.

Keeping the gun jammed into Kate's ribs, the woman yanked off the ski mask and long, fluffy blond hair spilled around her shoulders. Kate studied the woman's fine-boned face, and a niggle of recognition teased her brain.

"I see by your expression that you recognize me," the woman said and shrugged. "No matter. We want the senator to know exactly who was behind what happened today and why."

"The senator?" A chill spun through Kate.

"That's right. It's not you we want. You're a tool. A means to an end. If you cooperate, you'll be home, baking your pies and cakes, in a few hours." As she hustled Kate down the street, the woman shoved the ski mask in a coat pocket.

Baking her pies and cakes? Kate shivered. Whoever these people were, they knew who she was, knew what she did for a living. But how? And what made her their "tool"?

"Keep moving, Betty Crocker, and don't try anything stupid like running from me. You can't outrun a bullet, and I have orders to kill you if you give me trouble."

Fear slithered down Kate's spine, and she sucked in a deep breath of the cold damp air, fighting to keep her wits about her.

"This way," the woman ordered, grabbing Kate's arm and dragging her farther down the street with the gun discreetly hidden in her coat pocket but aimed at Kate's back.

Gage had seen the woman take her. Would he come after her to help her or would his duty to Hank Kelley be his priority? With a sinking sensation in her gut, Kate realized Gage had answered that question many times already. His job came first, at all costs.

But the bank tellers and other witnesses…surely someone had summoned the police to help her. She just had to stay calm, keep a clear head until she knew how the woman planned to use her, how she fitted in these peoples' scheme.

When her feet slipped on dry leaves on the sidewalk, Kate stumbled, and her captor's grip tightened on her arm.

"I'm warning you," the woman grated, "no tricks!"

"No, I didn't—"

"In here." Before Kate could catch her breath, the woman shoved her toward the door of a vacant building. A faded sign that hung drunkenly over the door read, Sue's Alterations. A fist-sized hole in the door's window and the fact that her captor was able to open the door unimpeded told her this hideout had been preplanned.

Would anyone think to look for her in this abandoned shop? Kate's heart beat a panicked rhythm. Her feet rooted to the sidewalk, and when the woman nudged her, directing her inside, she balked. She cast a frantic glance up and down the windswept street, searching for anyone she could signal, someone who would help her.

"Move it!" her captor growled, giving her a shove.

As she lost the battle, her knees buckling under the force of the woman's push, she glimpsed a tall figure darting out of the bank's back door, the same door she'd been dragged through moments earlier. She knew that dark hair and those broad shoulders....

Hope fired in her chest.

"Gage!" she shouted as she stumbled inside the dilapidated store front.

Gage snapped his gaze in the direction the shout had come and caught a brief glimpse of a dark coat disappearing into a building a couple of blocks down the street. He sprinted down the sidewalk, leading with the security guard's .38 revolver. His senses tingled, hyperalert as he passed alleys and parked cars, all too aware that an ambush could be waiting behind any blind corner.

Every blown leaf and icy howl of wind had his nerves

jangling, and he forced himself to breathe deeply through his nose as he raced down the street. Echoes of gunfire and exploding IEDs ricocheted through his brain, taunting him. The last time the stakes had been this high, the last time he'd had someone else's life in his hands, he'd failed. Spectacularly.

Adrenaline spiked his pulse and sent a tremor through his limbs.

Stop it! Focus. Concentrate.

He couldn't let his jumpiness interfere with helping Kate. Couldn't let his last screw up taint this rescue.

When he reached the area where he'd seen the flash of movement, Gage slowed his pace, the gun ready, and sidled up to the front wall of the building to hide his approach. He crept to the corner of a barber shop and peered in the front window. The only person inside was the elderly barber, who snoozed in the reclining chair.

He edged to the next storefront. Except for the front door, the building's windows were boarded. The glass in the door was broken, the lock damaged. Someone had broken in.

His body tensing, he inched forward. He stayed behind the boarded windows, out of sight. Listening. Craning his neck to see the inside the dark store.

Over the whistling wind, he heard women's voices. One was Kate's. The other...?

Did the kidnapper have another hostage?

He tested the door with his toe. It creaked open.

"Who's there?" the other woman shouted.

Damn! They'd heard the door. So much for the element of surprise.

"Gage?" Kate cried, then gasped audibly.

He hazarded a better look in the room. Just a quick peek that yielded a plethora of information. The kidnapper was the other woman. Kate was being held in the back corner of the shop with a gun to her head.

The abandoned shop still had a cash counter, a workbench of some kind, rolling wardrobe racks. Instantly he began calculating. Planning.

With a deep breath to steel himself, center his focus, Gage kicked open the door and swung inside. "Drop your weapon!"

Both Kate and the woman gave startled screams.

Gage darted behind the counter. With both hands steadying the .38, he took careful aim on the woman holding Kate. "Let her go."

The woman, an attractive blonde, probably in her forties, flinched. Her face looked familiar. Alarms sounded in Gage's mind.

"No! Stay back!" She scooted away, dragging Kate with her until their backs bumped the far wall. Gage heard panic in the woman's voice, and the hand holding the gun on Kate trembled.

His gut tightened at seeing Kate at the business end of the bank robber's weapon. The woman's jittery manner told Gage she was no professional criminal. That thought should have comforted him. Instead, the woman's behavior made him more uneasy. She could be more unpredictable, more desperate to save herself, more irrational.

And where was the man who'd taken the wallets? Was he lying in wait, ready to ambush Gage?

"Release her. You don't want to add murder to the charges against you." Gage fought to keep his tone even and calmly commanding while everything inside him rioted at the notion of Kate getting hurt.

The situation had too many variables, too many oddities, too many unanswered questions. And Kate was caught in the middle. A prime setup for disaster. A cold sweat beaded on Gage's face.

"Who are you? What do you want?" His voice held a hard edge, and the woman shifted nervously.

"I'm the person who'll kill your girlfriend if you come any closer. *You* put *your* gun down and your hands up, or I'll shoot her. I will!" The blonde's tone was growing more shrill.

Gage held firm, mentally recalculating, when the woman's wording registered. *Your girlfriend.*

Ice shot through him. A multitude of questions buzzed through his head in a numb heartbeat. How did this woman know of his association with Kate? Was this more than a random act of theft and violence? Was this a personal attack directed at him? At Kate?

Was Janet involved? Larry? Was this a setup?

The possibility seemed too unlikely, too coincidental…

Yet…the woman did seem familiar somehow. Her voice…

"It's a trap, Ga—"

"Shut up!" The woman jammed the muzzle closer to Kate's ear.

A trap? Another wave of disquiet rippled through him.

Hank hadn't planned to go to the bank today until he'd received that text message… From his mercenary's phone….

Damn it!

Gage flicked a glance to Kate. Her gaze was riveted on him, her eyes bright with fear and…faith. *In him.*

His heart somersaulted. Doubt burrowed to the bone. How could she put her trust in him when his recent track record was so dismal?

I'm falling in love with you, too.

He blinked hard, yanking himself back to the situation at hand. He had to stay focused. He couldn't let his emotions cloud his actions.

Or had he already?

"A trap?" He narrowed his eyes on the woman, studying her windblown hair and familiar face hard, searching his memory….

A press conference on TV. One of Hank's mistresses

crying at the microphone. A woman's shrill voice squawking through Hank's cell.

Gage stiffened. "You're Gloria. Gloria Cosgrove."

Confusion and panic erupted inside the bank the minute Gage disappeared through the side door. Hank pressed a hand to the spot where acid sawed his gut. Weeks of stress and too much whiskey had given him a case of heartburn that felt like a heart attack, and the anxious cries of the women in the bank didn't help.

"Senator Kelley, in here!" a bank manager called from one of the offices. "I've called the police, but until they get here, you'll be safer to wait in here."

A few of the patrons hurried out of the bank, while others rushed to the protective walls of the employee offices. Tellers scurried in a crouch to secure the vault and assist customers to safety.

Damn it! Where had Prescott gone? Armed men had robbed him, and his bodyguard had done nothing but run after his girlfriend, abandoning him during the crisis. Such dereliction of duty was grounds for dismissal in Hank's book.

"Senator Kelley, your security man said to wait in an office," the manager called again, waving toward the open door behind him. "Please, sir. In here!"

Hank straightened his tie, and, as he headed toward the bank manager's office, he thought of his Town Car waiting outside. His car had bullet-resistant windows and doors. In his opinion, that made his Town Car safer than the manager's office.

He stopped in front of the manager and handed him the withdrawal slip and the note with the mercenary's account number. "I need you to transfer these funds from my account to the one I've written here. Today. It's a matter of utmost urgency."

"I—of course, sir."

"And tell Mr. Prescott I'm waiting for him in my car." With that, he headed for the front door and stepped outside into the blustery day. Despite the scare with the amateur bank robbers taking his wallet—he needed to call Cindy and tell her to cancel his credit cards—he was relieved to have the payoff to Garrison handled. The man was highly recommended, and it would be worth the price to see Lana rescued.

Hank sighed contentedly. Lana was as good as free, and once she was safely at the ranch with him, he'd tell the Raven's Head Society to leave him the hell alone.

Ducking his head against the cold wind, he marched toward his car, giving a cursory side-to-side glance around him for signs of trouble. Dark gray clouds gathered over the mountains, promising bad weather to come.

"Senator Kelley?" someone behind him said.

He stopped, huddling deeper in his coat as an icy gust buffeted him, and turned to see who'd spoken. "Yes?"

He saw the man in the dark overcoat, and a chill that had nothing to do with the encroaching storm blasted through him. Hank glanced down at the gun aimed at his chest and stumbled backward.

The man rushed forward, overtaking him in two long strides and jamming the gun in his ribs. "I need you to come with me. We have business to take care of."

Gloria Cosgrove's head swivelled toward Gage, her expression stunned. "How'd you know who I—" Then, with a scoff, she firmed her jaw and raised her chin. "Well. You're pretty smart. Is that why Hank hired you?"

Hank! Nausea swamped Gage, and he bit out a scorching curse.

"I see you've figured out our ploy," Gloria chortled.

He'd left Hank to follow the kidnapper. Abandoned his duty to rescue a bystander. Forsaken a U.S. Senator to come after Kate.

Because he loved her...

That truth stole the air from his lungs.

"While you're here saving your honey, the good senator is exposed, vulnerable. By now, my friends have found him." Gloria gave Gage a purely evil smile. "And taught him what happens to traitors to our cause."

His mistakes sat on his chest like boulders. Gage fought for a breath. Black spots swarmed his peripheral vision. He'd failed...*twice.* Not only had he let his emotions sidetrack him from his duty to the senator, but he'd let Kate past his private defenses. His weakness for her had given her false hope that they could have a future together, that she could trust him, that he'd protect her from getting hurt.

Furious with himself for falling for Gloria's trick, yet still worried sick about what Hank's scorned lover might do to Kate, Gage scrambled for a plan. He had to disarm Gloria, free Kate and get back to Hank. Like, ten minutes ago.

"Fine," Gage grated. "You fooled me. Now let Kate go. She's an innocent in this. You don't want to hurt her."

Innocent. And yet, because of her involvement with him, she'd been tainted, put in jeopardy. Proof positive he needed to get out of her life and leave her the hell alone.

Gloria shrugged. "Irrelevant collateral damage is always a sad fact in a war. You're a soldier. You know that."

Fear tripped down Gage's spine. "Kate is not irrelevant. If you hurt her, I'll—"

"What? Come on, tough guy, make your move!" Gloria taunted, growing bolder.

Wind rattled the metal awning of the deserted shop, creating a rumble like distant thunder, and his heart pounded an answering drumbeat.

Should he force Gloria's hand?

He resighted his weapon on Gloria, aiming for her gun arm—

And hesitated. If he shot Gloria and, in pain, shock or a physiological response, her finger tightened on the trigger, Kate would die.

Gage had no time to waste. He had to find Hank before—

Bang!

He jerked at the all-too-familiar noise. Then Kate's wail of agony rent the echoing concussions, and Gage's heart stilled.

"Who are you? What do you want?" Hank demanded as the bank robber hustled him at gunpoint into an alley and through a weatherbeaten door.

"I'd think by now it'd be obvious who we are, or at least who we work for." He shoved Hank forward, into the unlit room, and two more men stepped out of the shadows.

Hank squinted, trying to make out their faces, but he didn't recognize them. "I don't know what you—"

Before he could finish, the two men grabbed him by the arms, and the bank robber landed a breath-stealing blow to his gut. Pain ricocheted through him, and his knees buckled.

"We have a message for you from the Raven's Head Society, Senator."

Hank raised his head, gasping for air, and leveled a challenging glare on his tormenter. "Go to hell," he rasped.

The thug chuckled darkly. "You weren't smart to defy the members of the Society by sending that mercenary after your daughter. In case you're wondering, he failed to rescue her."

Hank shook his head. "You're lying. I heard from him this morning. He's ready to move in."

"He just needed his payment sent to an account in the Caymans by eleven," the man finished for him and pulled out a cell phone. "I know. He texted you at breakfast, right?"

Cold seeped to Hank's core. "You— The robbery was—"

"A setup. Yes. We had to get your bodyguard out of the way long enough to have our…chat."

"You sonofa—" Hank struggled against the grip of the two thugs but to no avail.

Stepping closer, the bank robber slammed his fist into Hank's jaw, followed by another swift jab in the gut. "Do I have your attention now?"

Bile rose in Hank's throat, and he wheezed.

"You know what you have to do to get Lana back. Cooperate with the Society, do as you've been instructed, and Lana will be returned. Defy us again, and things will get really nasty for you. They're not above killing your daughter if you don't comply."

Hank spat out the blood in his mouth and sent his captor another defiant glare.

The man in the dark coat sighed as if dealing with a petulant child, then loosed another attack on Hank's ribs, his kidneys, his face. When Hank crumpled to the cold concrete floor of the old storeroom, the men took turns kicking him.

The edges of his vision wavered and grew dim. Pain screamed from every muscle and bone in his body.

"You can't hide on your son's ranch forever," the man growled in Hank's ear. "Consider this your last warning."

Chapter 14

Kate collapsed on the floor, a searing ache exploding in her thigh. No sooner had she hit the floor than another ear-shattering blast echoed through the room.

The woman—Gloria, Gage had called her—screamed in pain and dropped her gun. The weapon clattered to the floor beside Kate. Shoving aside her haze of pain and shock, Kate rallied her wits and scrambled to the gun, dragging it into her grasp.

She cut a side glance to Gloria, who was curled up on the floor clutching her bloody hand to her chest.

Gage darted around the counter and dropped to his knees beside her. "Lie still, sweetheart. I have to tie her up, then I'll find something to staunch the bleeding."

Her head still buzzing with adrenaline, Kate glanced at her leg and gasped. She gaped in horror at the hole in her flesh that seeped a steady trickle of blood.

Biting the inside of her cheek, she swallowed the wail

of agony and fear that welled in her throat. She had to stay strong. Gage didn't need the distraction of her breaking down while he dealt with Gloria.

Following his directions, Kate rolled to her back, tears prickling her eyes. She fought to steady her breathing, calm her racing pulse. Gage was here. She would be all right....

Turning her head to the side, she watched numbly as he used the belt from Gloria's coat to tie her wrists together and secure them to a heavy metal rack. The woman whimpered and groaned in pain, her face deathly pale and her hand severely damaged by Gage's well-placed shot.

"It hurts..." Gloria moaned.

"You should have thought of that before you put that gun to Kate's head," Gage growled. He took out his cell and dialed. "I need an ambulance and the police in downtown Maple Cove."

As he gave directions to the operator, Gage grabbed the scarf Kate wore draped around her neck and wrapped it in a tight tourniquet around her leg. He worked quickly, efficiently, his expression intensely focused. Then he used both hands to apply pressure to her wound.

She yelped as lightning pain streaked though her.

Worried blue eyes found hers briefly, and he rasped, "I'm sorry. I know you must be in agony, but I have to push on the wound to stop the bleeding."

She gritted her teeth and swallowed against the nausea that swamped her. Instead of the throb in her leg, she centered her attention on Gage, the fine lines of stress and concern framing his eyes.

"You came for me. Saved me," she whispered.

His gazed darted back to hers. Stunned. Guilty. Grief-stricken. "Of course I did." He paused, and a muscle in his jaw twitched as he clenched his teeth. "I love you."

Kate felt a hot tear leak onto her cheek. "Then give me a chance to love you back."

Silently, Gage held her gaze for several taut seconds. Only when the whine of an approaching siren splintered the quiet did he jerk his gaze away and shove to his feet.

Without answering her, he hurried to the door to flag down the ambulance. He stood back as the EMTs bustled in, and he gave the medics a bullet-point recap of what had happened.

Pointing to Gloria, he said, "Keep her restrained until the police come. She's to be charged with kidnapping, armed robbery and attempted murder." Shifting his gaze to Kate, he said quietly, "I'll check on you at the hospital later, but I have to go now. I have to find the senator. Pray I'm not too late."

Kate's heart lurched as Gage disappeared through the door. His parting words reverberated in her head. He'd put her life ahead of that of a U.S. Senator.

Of course I did. I love you. Her heart twisted. He'd had a terrible choice to make, between duty and love. And he'd chosen her. Perhaps at the expense of an important man's life.

Gage had a dangerous, critically important job. How could she expect him to give even a second thought to a relationship with her when he had responsibility for a man's life, possibly even matters of national security to handle? She couldn't.

Yet at dinner last night she'd pressed him for a commitment. Remorse settled in her chest like a rock. She'd been so selfish!

She bit the inside of her cheek, fighting back tears of pain and regret as the EMTs moved her onto a gurney and bumped her across the threshold to the waiting ambulance.

One of the medics held a syringe up for her to see. "This is for pain. Do you have any allergies?"

She shook her head and welcomed the relief the drug brought her as it was injected in her IV. But as her head grew woozy and her eyelids drooped from the sedating pain-killer, she wished there was an equally effective remedy for her broken heart.

Gage's pulse pounded with the drumbeat of guilt as he crept into the dank alley. Leading with the security guard's weapon, he swept his gaze over the scattered trash and the collection of dead leaves that littered the narrow gap between the old buildings.

When he had reached the bank after leaving Kate, the manager had explained that Hank had gone to the car to wait. Except, no one was at the car.

Castigating himself for his screw up, Gage had begun searching the streets, asking in the businesses along the thoroughfare for witnesses, tips…*anything* to tell him where the senator might be. Calls to Hank's secure cell went unanswered. No one remembered seeing him. He was gone. Just… gone.

Gage was about to turn and move on from the alley when a faint moan filtered through the chill air. He stood motionless and listened, trying to pinpoint the source.

Despite the autumn cold, Gage's palm sweated around the revolver's grip. His gut knotted when he thought of how he'd been duped, how his mistake might have cost Senator Kelley his life.

But how could he have turned his back on Kate knowing her life was in jeopardy? He gritted his teeth as he prowled toward the back of the alley. He'd known what his involvement with Kate could mean to his job, the heartache he'd leave Kate with, but he'd not imagined the danger to Hank would reach Kate. His relationship with her, his feelings for her had become a liability to her in the worst possible way.

Another muffled groan pulled him from his self-incriminations and drew him to a weathered door with rusty hinges. Gage tested the knob, and with a creak, the door was caught by the chill October wind and swung open. Gage flattened himself against the alley wall beside the door. He carefully scanned the room, his gun aimed into the darkness, before he ventured inside.

Huddled in the fetal position on the floor, Senator Kelley clutched his stomach and moaned in misery. Bitter compunction rose in Gage's throat. Hank's face was beaten and bleeding, and Gage could only blame his own miscalculation and distraction.

Continuing his visual search of the dark room, Gage edged inside. When he was certain no one lurked in the shadows, he knelt beside Hank and began a field assessment of the man's injuries. "Senator Kelley, how badly are you hurt?"

"No…more," the man croaked.

Gage loosened Hank's tie and eased him onto his back. "Senator, it's Gage. What happened? Who did this?"

Hank opened his eyes a slit, and when he saw his bodyguard, he visibly wilted. Relief softened the tension in his face. "Raven's Head…warning…"

Ice shot through Gage. Knowing that the senator's enemies had found a way to get to Hank and could have killed him sent fresh waves of frustration and guilt deep into Gage's soul. "Can you walk, sir? We need to get you to the hospital."

Hank gazed up at him with bleary eyes. "The waitress… Kate…"

Gage tensed, prepared for Hank's condemnation, for the senator's censure for Gage failing his duty to his client.

But Hank surprised him, narrowing a concerned look through puffy, bruised eyes. "Did they…hurt her?"

"Sir?"

"Did you…find her? Help her?"

Acid churned through Gage when he thought of having left Kate, still bleeding, still in agony from her gunshot wound.

He swallowed hard. "The second gunman was Gloria Cosgrove, sir."

Hank's expression reflected his shock.

"She shot Kate in the leg, but I was able to subdue Gloria until the ambulance arrived for Kate. The cops should have been right behind them."

Hank groaned and closed his eyes with a wince. "Will Kate be…all right?" The rasp of his voice was growing fainter. Clearly Hank needed medical attention—and fast. Yet his determination to find out about Kate's condition, his thoughts of someone besides himself while he lay bleeding and battered touched Gage. Maybe the senator wasn't a lost cause after all.

Gage dug his cell phone out of his pocket and dialed 911. "She's on her way to the hospital now. She should be all right."

At least he prayed she'd make a full recovery. More than anything he wanted to be at her side right now, holding her hand, encouraging her. But his duty was to Hank, and he'd already failed the senator in a big way.

When the emergency operator answered, he gave her the lowdown on Hank's condition and location, ordering another ambulance, stat. When he was told how long it would take the lone ambulance in the area to take the women to the hospital in Honey Creek and come back for Hank, Gage changed his mind. "I'll drive him then. But tell the hospital that the patient is Senator Henry Kelley, and he's been savagely attacked by unknown assailants. Notify his family to meet us there and have extra security standing by."

Gage drove as fast as felt safe, checking the rearview mirror to keep tabs on Hank, who lay sprawled on the back seat, wincing every time the Town Car hit a bump. Gage was pretty certain Hank had no broken limbs, but his ribs had taken a beating and could be cracked.

At the Honey Creek hospital, they were met outside the E.R. by an orderly and a nurse with a gurney. Two Honey Creek sheriff's deputies stood sentinel by the admitting door and followed Hank as he was wheeled inside. In the E.R. driveway, Gage spotted the ambulance that had brought Kate and Gloria in, and his chest tightened.

Please let Kate be all right.

A young, sandy haired doctor in scrubs and a white lab coat hurried over to Hank and made a cursory assessment of his condition. "Take him to exam room three."

When Gage fell in step to follow Hank's gurney, the young doctor caught his arm. "Whoa, partner. Where do you think you're going?"

"I'm his bodyguard. Where he goes, I go."

The sandy haired man, whose lab coat bore the name Dr. Finn Colton, arched an eyebrow, as if to say, *And where were you when this man was taking a beating?*

"Colton?" Gage said. "Any relation to the sheriff?"

"Brother. Why?"

"Just curious. I met Wes last week when he investigated a breach of the security system at the Kelley ranch."

Dr. Colton nodded once. "Listen, normally I ask the family to wait out here while I treat the patient…"

"I'm not family. I'm his bodyguard, and I need to be with him. I don't know who is after him and where they might have planted operatives."

"I can vouch for everyone on my staff."

"Just the same, I have a duty to protect the senator. I *am* going back."

Finn gave him a hard look then scowled. "All right, but make sure you stay out of our way."

As Gage and Dr. Colton headed back to the exam room,

Gage cast a glance into each room they passed, hoping to catch a glimpse of Kate. "Dr. Colton, are you aware of another patient that would have been brought in within the hour with a gunshot wound to the leg? Her name's Kate Rogers. She's a pretty blonde—"

Finn was nodding as they rounded the corner into exam room three where the nurses were checking Hank's vitals. "Just saw her."

Gage's stomach jumped. "How is she?"

"Is she family?" Finn asked, stepping over to shine a tiny flashlight in each of Hank's eyes. "'Cause, by law, I'm not allowed to talk about a patient's condition to anyone except immediate family."

"She's his wife," Hank croaked, surprising both Finn and Gage.

Finn sent a skeptical look to Gage for confirmation, and Gage frowned. He couldn't lie, even if it meant knowing the truth about Kate. "I'm just a friend, but...she means a great deal to me."

Hank groaned, though whether in disgust with Gage's honesty or pain from his injuries, Gage couldn't say. Probably the former.

Dr. Colton continued his examination of Hank's injuries, murmuring an order to the nurse to contact radiology to set up a chest X-ray, before glancing back at Gage. "Sorry, I can't help you. You can talk to her yourself later. I've asked that she be admitted overnight for observation."

"And the other woman, Gloria Cosgrove. She had a GSW to her hand. Are you keeping her here? She'll need a full-time guard on her, if you do."

"I believe she's already been treated and released into police custody."

"Your brother's men or the Maple Cove department?"

Finn paused from his work and furrowed his brow in thought. "I believe it was an officer from Maple Cove."

Gage gritted his teeth. He'd have much preferred that Sheriff Wes Colton and his men handled the case. Based on how the Maple Cove PD had responded to Janet's domestic abuse situation, he didn't trust the small-town yahoos to cross all the t's and dot all the i's with Gloria.

When Dr. Colton finished his exam, he promised to check in with them again once Hank had been X-rayed and the films came back. The hospital personnel whisked out of the room, leaving Gage and Hank alone in the exam room.

Gage took a chair beside Hank's gurney and rubbed his face with both hands. *Geez, what a day.*

"So go see her," Hank croaked.

Gage raised his head and furrowed his brow. "What?"

Hank met his gaze through puffy eyes. "Kate. I know... you're worried about her."

Clenching his teeth and battling down the swell of emotion in his throat, Gage said, "You're my responsibility. I left you earlier and look at you."

"Not your fault. They'd...have found a way...to get me with or...without you." Hank closed his eyes and sighed slowly, wincing. "Do you...love her?"

Gage frowned and shifted in the hard seat, uncomfortable with the direct question. He didn't want to discuss Kate with anyone, especially not Hank. "You should be resting."

The senator grunted. "Do you...love her?"

Gage flexed and balled his hand, fidgeting. "Maybe. Doesn't matter now." The memory of Kate's hurt and disappointment last night arrowed through Gage. "We have no future together."

"Why not?"

He scowled at Hank. Why hadn't the painkillers they'd

given him knocked him out yet? Why the third degree from Hank all of the sudden?

"I don't want to talk about it."

"Well, I do." Hank sent him a stern look. "'Cause you're being…an idiot."

Gage raised an eyebrow. "You really want to go there?"

"Yeah, I know. I'm one…to talk. But that's no…excuse for you to act the fool."

Gage puffed out a deep breath through pursed lips. Fine. He'd lay out the facts for Hank, and then maybe the guy would drop the subject. "All right, yes, I love her. She's kind and smart and beautiful and full of joy and hope. When I'm with her, I feel happier than I have in years."

Hank opened his mouth to reply, and Gage cut him off. "But…" He drew his brow into a frown. "I'm all wrong for her. Breaking things off with her was the best thing I could do for her. We're opposites, Kate and I, and I don't want her to look back in a few years and realize I've dragged her down, held her back, sucked all the joy out of her life."

"Who says…you would?"

Gage scoffed. "Look at me. I'm an ex-Ranger who screwed up his last mission and watched his whole team die. I have nightmares about the sounds and sights of that day. I jump at loud noises and carry around a boatload of guilt."

"So talk to a shrink."

He shook his head. "I don't need a shrink."

"Ah. You'd rather…wallow in your misery."

Gage sent Hank a dirty look.

"You hold on to your guilt, because you lived…and your team didn't."

"Damn right! It was my fault they died! Scouting the route was my job, and I failed!" Gage surged to his feet to pace. As little as he wanted to talk about Kate, he wanted to discuss his last mission in Afghanistan even less.

"Oh." Hank nodded. "So you don't think…you deserve to be happy now. You think…your being happy disrespects… the tragedy of losing your team?"

"I didn't say that." Yet Hank's assessment needled him. Was that why he couldn't commit to Kate?

Hank was quiet for a moment, his eyes closed, and Gage prayed that meant the painkillers had finally helped him fall asleep. In the lull of conversation, Gage squeezed the bridge of his nose and worked hard to rein in the riot of emotions bubbling inside him. He didn't need to be grilled like this after all the turbulence of the day. He was too raw, too tired…

"Kate…makes you happy…but you pushed her away."

Great. The inquisitor was still awake.

Gage sighed impatiently. "Because I don't want to hurt her."

"And how…would you do that?"

"Look at me. I'm a mess, and I can only be a drain on her life. She deserves more."

"Or…" Hank met his gaze, and Gage jolted at the lucidity still sparking in his eyes. "She could be just what you need… to move past your guilt and…make a fresh start."

Let my love heal you. We can work through whatever happened to you together, if you'd let me help. Gage gritted his teeth, fighting the tremors that raced through him, shoving down the hope that filled his chest like a balloon until he couldn't breathe.

"Do you…have any idea what I'd give…for a fresh start, a second chance with my family?" Hank's battered face filled with regret. "Love doesn't come…around every day. Don't blow it."

Gage sank back down on the hard chair, his heart heavy, his thoughts tangled. "I don't know."

"You have PTSD."

Gage jerked his head up. Post-traumatic stress disorder? He knew the term but had never applied it to what he was going through.

Hank drilled him with a hard, determined gaze. "Get… professional help." He paused, letting his suggestion—no, it had been an order, a plea—sink in. "Then you can…focus on what matters." Hank sounded groggier now, out of breath. "Love matters. Don't…lose it."

A knock sounded on the exam room door, and Cole stepped in from the hall. "Dad?" He took in his father's condition with a sweeping glance and paled. He muttered an obscenity under his breath and approached the side of the bed. "Who did this to you, Dad, and why? What's going on?"

Hank ignored Cole's question, holding Gage's gaze. "Once you're…on your feet, focus…your energy on…making Kate happy. Giving her everything she deserves."

Gage's pulse tripped. Would he ever reach a point where he buoyed Kate's spirits and brought her the same joy and light she gave him? He wanted that so badly he could taste it. He wanted to pamper Kate and fill her life with love and happiness.

Cole jammed his hands in his pockets and divided a curious look between his father and Gage. "What happened to Kate?"

Hank raised an unsteady hand, signaling for Cole to wait. "Go see her. Tell her…how you feel. Don't lose her."

Gage hesitated. "I can't leave you, while—"

"Cole's here. There are guards outside. I'm protected." A grin twitched at the corner of Hank's bloody lip. "Go. That's an order."

Gage shoved to his feet. Purpose and hope filled his stride as he crossed to the door. He glanced back at Cole, touching the cell phone clipped to his hip. "I'm just a call away if you need me." Then to Hank, "Thanks. While I'm gone—" he gave Cole another meaningful glance "—take your own advice. Make a fresh start."

A dull ache radiated from the gunshot wound in Kate's thigh as she stared at the ceiling above her hospital bed. The injection she'd received made the pain in her leg tolerable, but nothing seemed to ease the sting in her heart. She felt so alone, especially with Janet gone to Idaho. When tears threatened, she blinked them back, refusing to feel sorry for herself. She had so much to be grateful for. Determined to keep her spirits up, she reviewed her blessings. Janet was free of Larry, safe in another state and making a new start for herself. The bullet had missed vital blood vessels and bone and had passed through her leg, meaning her recovery would be much quicker.

And Gage…

Her heart sank again. What was she supposed to do about Gage?

And suddenly he was at her door, as if her thoughts had conjured him. He gave a soft knock then said softly, "Kate? May I come in?"

"O-of course." She struggled to sit up, then gasped when a sharp twinge shot through her leg.

Gage was at her side in an instant, catching her shoulders and easing her back against her pillows. "Hey, take it easy. Are you okay? Can I get you anything?"

She shook her head. "How's the senator? No one will tell me anything."

With a guilty grimace, Gage caught her up on the senator's condition.

"Have they caught the men responsible for attacking him? Gloria's accomplices?" she asked.

He shrugged. "Not as far as I know."

"Then what are you doing here? Shouldn't you be protecting Senator Kelley?"

"Cole is with him, and…the senator is the one who sent me to see you."

Kate stilled. Did the senator blame her for drawing Gage away from him?

Gage must have read her confusion, because the corner of his mouth twitched in a brief grin, and he wrapped his fingers around her hand. The warmth of his large, calloused hand surrounding hers made her heart kick with longing.

He took a deep breath and expelled it. "Senator Kelley thinks I have PTSD."

She frowned. "Post-traumatic stress?"

He nodded, and her mind clicked through the past two weeks. His grimness, his reluctance to talk about his past, and… "Last week when the truck backfired outside the diner…"

Gage nodded again and sent her an embarrassed half grin. "I've been in denial, not wanting to put a name to it, but the truth is I have flashbacks, nightmares…guilt."

She squeezed his hand. "Gage…"

Holding up his free hand to halt her, he swallowed hard and said, "It was my last mission in Afghanistan…."

For the next several minutes, he told her a horrific story of death and destruction and loss. As he talked, Kate realized what reliving the experience cost him. Realized why he was telling her. His revelation of his trauma was a gift to her, an expression of his trust in her, a sacrificial gesture meant to bridge the gulf between them.

While her heart ached for his suffering, for the guilt he'd heaped on himself, another part of her, deep in her soul, rejoiced. By unburdening himself for her, he'd taken the first step in healing, made the first move toward building an open, honest relationship.

"When I got back stateside, the army offered me psychiatric services, but I refused them. I thought I could handle it alone. But..." He paused and shook his head. "Hank...Senator Kelley thinks if I see a counselor now, I can still sort through my guilt and get past the nightmares that haunt me."

She held her breath, not daring to interrupt him. She offered her support by taking his other hand in hers, stroking his knuckles with her thumb.

"He thinks I'm punishing myself for my team's deaths by not letting myself be happy, not letting you love me."

Kate's heart clenched. "Oh, Gage..."

"He thinks I should give my love for you a chance."

A beat of expectant silence passed before she risked asking, "And what do *you* think?"

"I think..." Gage paused, then slipped one hand from her grasp to wipe the collection of moisture from his eyes. "I think he's right." He brought her hand to his lips for a kiss. "I love you, Kate, and I want the chance to make you as happy as you make me."

Tears blurred her vision as she laughed and cried at the same time. "You already make me happy, Gage. You show you care in so many ways. And you helped me get Janet free of Larry when no one else would."

He smiled brighter, blinking and clearing his throat, obviously struggling with emotions he didn't know how to express. Then he jerked his chin up and sent her a puzzled frown. "Wait, say that last part again? Are you saying—?"

"Janet and Larry had another big fight last night. He hit her again, and she came to my house. I...didn't let her in." Kate wet her lips, still having mixed feelings about her act of tough love.

Gage reached for her cheek and stroked his fingers along her jaw. "And?"

"Something we'd been telling her must have finally sunk in. She drove herself to a women's shelter somewhere in Idaho. I don't know where, but when she called this morning she sounded...relieved to be free of him." Kate released a sigh. "For the first time in years, I'm not worried about my sister. I know she'll find her feet and make a great new life for herself."

He nodded and lifted the corner of his mouth. "That's good. Really good."

She bit her lip and tilted her head, voicing the idea she'd only been toying with before now. "I think I'll take the Kelleys up on their offer to work for Kelley's Cookhouse in Honey Creek. It's a great opportunity."

"You'll be great at it. How could you not be? You have baking talent to spare." His grin faded a degree, and he arched an eyebrow. "But will you have time to spare with your new job? Time to, say...date? Time to get to know a certain ex-Ranger better and build the foundation of a lasting relationship?"

Joy burst into bloom, filling Kate's chest and bringing a wide smile to her face. "I think the question is, how will I find time for the job? I plan to spend a lot of time with the man I love, planning our future."

"Becoming a family," he added, and her heart skipped a beat. As he leaned close and pressed a kiss to her lips, a warmth wrapped around her, a sense of belonging and home. With Gage, she knew she'd found what her heart longed for most.

"Yes," she said on a sigh, *"our* family."

Epilogue

"The vultures are circling," Cole said the next afternoon with a sigh of disgust as he stomped in from the cold and hung his coat on a peg by the front door. Outside, bright sunshine belied the bite in the air, the dropping temperatures that could spell trouble for Cole's herd if the snow predicted in a few days arrived.

"Vultures?" Hannah sent her boss a querying glance.

"The paparazzi camped out at the ranch entrance." Cole glanced to the couch where his father was propped on several pillows with an ice pack on his cheek. "Were they out there when Gage brought you home from the hospital this morning?"

"Afraid so." Hank readjusted the ice pack and closed his eyes. "News of the attack on me was leaked from the hospital. Didn't take long for the media to show up, looking for the story."

"Needless to say, I don't want anyone talking to the press."

Gage echoed his warning by dividing a stern glance among everyone present.

Hannah nodded. "Goes without saying." She directed her attention to Cole. "Did you offer Rusty a room in the main house for his recuperation?"

Cole dropped into a stuffed chair and raked his hair with his fingers. "I did. He said he'd be fine at his own place."

"Then he's all settled in? Does he need anything?" Hannah asked.

"He's settling in. I told him to call the house anytime if he needed help." Cole dropped his gaze to the floor, and his voice grew softer. "When I left him, he was calling Bethany."

"Bethany?" Gage looked to the others for clarification.

"His daughter in Chicago," Hannah supplied, though her gaze was on Cole, her expression expectant, worried.

Gage was deciding whether to ask why Bethany was a source of concern to Hannah when his phone rang. His heart leaped, knowing it could be Kate calling to set a time for him to come by her house that evening. He'd had Bart cover for him long enough to escort Kate home from the hospital and get her situated on her couch with the remote and plenty of snacks. Being short-staffed, the diner had closed temporarily, giving Laurie the opportunity to sit with Kate until Gage could bring in dinner and spend the night helping her deal with her injured leg. The first night of many he planned to spend cuddled close to the woman of his dreams.

But the number on his cell was not Kate's. The caller ID read, Honey Creek Sheriff Dept.

"Prescott? Wes Colton here. Has anyone from the Maple Cove PD called you today?"

Gage frowned. "No. Why?"

Sheriff Colton hesitated. "I have bad news."

His stomach swooping in dread, Gage mentally braced himself. "Go on."

"They don't know how, and they lost video surveillance that would tell them when… In fact, the whole scenario is baffling…alarming, but…"

Gage tensed. "Just tell me what happened."

Wes Colton sighed his frustration. "Somehow, last night, Gloria Cosgrove escaped without a trace from the Maple Cove jail."

* * * * *

Harlequin®

ROMANTIC
SUSPENSE

COMING NEXT MONTH

Available August 30, 2011

You can find more information on upcoming
Harlequin® titles, free excerpts and more at
www.HarlequinInsideRomance.com.

REQUEST YOUR FREE BOOKS!
2 FREE NOVELS PLUS 2 FREE GIFTS!

ROMANTIC
SUSPENSE
Sparked by Danger, Fueled by Passion.

YES! Please send me 2 FREE Harlequin® Romantic Suspense novels and my 2 FREE gifts (gifts are worth about $10). After receiving them, if I don't wish to receive any more books, I can return the shipping statement marked "cancel." If I don't cancel, I will receive 4 brand-new novels every month and be billed just $4.49 per book in the U.S. or $5.24 per book in Canada. That's a saving of at least 14% off the cover price! It's quite a bargain! Shipping and handling is just 50¢ per book in the U.S. and 75¢ per book in Canada.* I understand that accepting the 2 free books and gifts places me under no obligation to buy anything. I can always return a shipment and cancel at any time. Even if I never buy another book, the two free books and gifts are mine to keep forever.

240/340 HDN FEFR

Name	(PLEASE PRINT)

Address	Apt. #

City	State/Prov.	Zip/Postal Code

Signature (if under 18, a parent or guardian must sign)

Mail to the **Reader Service**:
IN U.S.A.: P.O. Box 1867, Buffalo, NY 14240-1867
IN CANADA: P.O. Box 609, Fort Erie, Ontario L2A 5X3

Not valid for current subscribers to Harlequin Romantic Suspense books.

Want to try two free books from another line?
Call 1-800-873-8635 or visit www.ReaderService.com.

* Terms and prices subject to change without notice. Prices do not include applicable taxes. Sales tax applicable in N.Y. Canadian residents will be charged applicable taxes. Offer not valid in Quebec. This offer is limited to one order per household. All orders subject to credit approval. Credit or debit balances in a customer's account(s) may be offset by any other outstanding balance owed by or to the customer. Please allow 4 to 6 weeks for delivery. Offer available while quantities last.

Your Privacy—The Reader Service is committed to protecting your privacy. Our Privacy Policy is available online at www.ReaderService.com or upon request from the Reader Service.

We make a portion of our mailing list available to reputable third parties that offer products we believe may interest you. If you prefer that we not exchange your name with third parties, or if you wish to clarify or modify your communication preferences, please visit us at www.ReaderService.com/consumerschoice or write to us at Reader Service Preference Service, P.O. Box 9062, Buffalo, NY 14269. Include your complete name and address.

HRS11B

New York Times *and* USA TODAY *bestselling author*
Maya Banks presents a brand-new miniseries

PREGNANCY & PASSION

When four irresistible tycoons face
the consequences of temptation.

Book 1—ENTICED BY HIS FORGOTTEN LOVER

Available September 2011 from Harlequin® Desire®!

Rafael de Luca had been in bad situations before. A crowded ballroom could never make him sweat.

These people would never know that he had no memory of any of them.

He surveyed the party with grim tolerance, searching for the source of his unease.

At first his gaze flickered past her, but he yanked his attention back to a woman across the room. Her stare bored holes through him. Unflinching and steady, even when his eyes locked with hers.

Petite, even in heels, she had a creamy olive complexion. A wealth of inky-black curls cascaded over her shoulders and her eyes were equally dark.

She looked at him as if she'd already judged him and found him lacking. He'd never seen her before in his life. Or had he?

He cursed the gaping hole in his memory. He'd been diagnosed with selective amnesia after his accident four months ago. Which seemed like complete and utter bull. No one got amnesia except hysterical women in bad soap operas.

With a smile, he disengaged himself from the group

around him and made his way to the mystery woman.

She wasn't coy. She stared straight at him as he approached, her chin thrust upward in defiance.

"Excuse me, but have we met?" he asked in his smoothest voice.

His gaze moved over the generous swell of her breasts pushed up by the empire waist of her black cocktail dress.

When he glanced back up at her face, he saw fury in her eyes.

"Have we *met?*" Her voice was barely a whisper, but he felt each word like the crack of a whip.

Before he could process her response, she nailed him with a right hook. He stumbled back, holding his nose.

One of his guards stepped between Rafe and the woman, accidentally sending her to one knee. Her hand flew to the folds of her dress.

It was then, as she cupped her belly, that the realization hit him. She was pregnant.

Her eyes flashing, she turned and ran down the marble hallway.

Rafael ran after her. He burst from the hotel lobby, and saw two shoes sparkling in the moonlight, twinkling at him.

He blew out his breath in frustration and then shoved the pair of sparkly, ultrafeminine heels at his head of security.

"Find the woman who wore these shoes."

Will Rafael find his mystery woman?
Find out in Maya Banks's passionate new novel
ENTICED BY HIS FORGOTTEN LOVER
Available September 2011 from Harlequin® Desire®!

Harlequin®

ROMANTIC
SUSPENSE

NEW YORK TIMES BESTSELLING AUTHOR
RACHEL LEE

The Rescue Pilot

Time is running out…

Desperate to help her ailing sister, Rory is determined
to get Cait the necessary treatment to help her fight
a devastating disease. A cross-country trip turns into
a fight for survival in more ways than one when their plane
encounters trouble. Can Rory trust pilot Chase Dakota
with their lives, and possibly her heart?

**Look for this heart-stopping romance in September
from *New York Times* bestselling author Rachel Lee
and Harlequin Romantic Suspense!**

Conard County THE NEXT GENERATION

Available in September wherever books are sold!

www.Harlequin.com.

RSRL27741